Gloved hands wrapped around her throat.

The hulk who had attacked Evan earlier had returned to finish the job and got her instead. He shoved her under the swirling water of the hot tub, growling that she'd cost him a lot of money and would regret it.

Fear exploded through her veins. This couldn't be the end. Not like this.

Kicking wildly, she fought him off and clawed her way out onto the deck. But he followed, this time wielding a knife.

"Jody!" She thought she dreamed the sound of Evan's voice. He raced across the deck, gun in hand. "Freeze," he yelled.

The hulk in black sprinted across the backyard. Evan didn't shoot or give chase. Instead, he ran to Jody and pulled her against his chest. "Are you hurt? Can—"

She broke away and looked into his eyes. "Evan, listen to me. You're in big trouble."

"Me? But you—"

She steadied herself as she uttered what she'd been fearing all along. "Someone put a hit out on you."

Jessica R. Patch lives in the mid-South, where she pens inspirational contemporary romance and romantic suspense novels. When she's not hunched over her laptop or going on adventurous trips with willing friends in the name of research, you can find her watching way too much Netflix with her family and collecting recipes to amazing dishes she'll probably never cook. To learn more about Jessica, please visit her at jessicarpatch.com.

Books by Jessica R. Patch

Love Inspired Suspense

The Security Specialists

Deep Waters
Secret Service Setup

Fatal Reunion
Protective Duty
Concealed Identity
Final Verdict

SECRET SERVICE SETUP

JESSICA R. PATCH

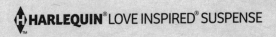
HARLEQUIN® LOVE INSPIRED® SUSPENSE

LOVE INSPIRED BOOKS

Recycling programs
for this product may
not exist in your area.

ISBN-13: 978-1-335-54365-3

Secret Service Setup

www.Harlequin.com

Printed in U.S.A.

We are troubled on every side, yet not distressed;
we are perplexed, but not in despair; Persecuted,
but not forsaken; cast down, but not destroyed.
– *2 Corinthians* 4:8-9

For my brother Jared. Remember that time we tied a rope
to the tail of our sister's stuffed cat and the railing on
the second floor, then swung across the stairs? We fell.
That inspired a scene in this book. Love you, little bro.

Special thanks to my agent Rachel Kent,
my editor Shana Asaro; Susan Tuttle, you're a brainstorming
rock star; Jodie Bailey, you got me unstuck with one simple
idea; Tiffany Capps for medical information (anything I
stretched for fiction is on me!); and to "Mr. Anonymous"
for helping me with a few Secret Service facts.

ONE

"Do you ever feel like sometimes the sunshine is deceiving because the day is going to be ominous regardless of how bright it is?" Jody Gallagher tapped her finger on the side of her Covenant Crisis Management coffee mug while her best friend and CCM's on-site psychologist, Cosette LaCroix, turned from the coffeepot, and her full lips—as red as the male cardinals outside—reminded Jody of a luscious makeup commercial.

"Is that how *you* feel?"

Jody should have known she'd get doctor-talk. *Was* that how she felt? A warm outer appearance, but cold inside? Maybe. She knew how to put up a good front. One could only whine and mourn over loss for so long before loved ones traded in supportiveness for speeches about moving on. Of course, said loved ones hadn't watched their dreams burn to ash right in front of their eyes.

In front of millions of eyes. She rubbed her temples. "I guess I'm dreading the day."

"At least he called and gave you fair warning he was coming." Cosette never said anything negative about the man Jody once loved—the man who'd single-handedly wrecked her dreams of someday becoming the youngest female Secret Service director. Dreams she'd birthed through spending time with her great-grandfather. She missed Granddaddy Flynn.

Jody-girl, one day you can be sitting right here in my chair. Doesn't have to be Wilder or any other boy. It can be you. I think it should be, darlin'. You can do anything you want. And if you want it, work for it. Do it. Achieve it.

She should have known better than to fall for a man who played hard—too hard. Especially after what she'd witnessed in Afghanistan. But she'd fallen for him. And he'd betrayed her. She'd been fired. Humiliated. Her reputation stained. Thankfully, Granddaddy Flynn hadn't lived to see that.

"Yeah, that was a bullet to the chest without any Kevlar kind of moment." To hear Evan Novak's voice after three years. She'd instantly recognized it—soft, smooth. Not a drop of grit until he laughed. He'd called to let her know he'd be in Atlanta today on protection detail for Senator Townes, who was campaigning for the primary election this coming November. A conservative in the South. Jody didn't expect trouble, but this morning she'd woken with a ball of tar coating her gut and it had spread since she'd rolled out of bed. Maybe it was the fact that she was going to see Evan. The Covenant Crisis team was leading the private security sector today and providing one of Georgia's wealthiest businessmen protection during the event—not that he needed it, but he was one of the largest campaign donors to Senator Townes, and if he wanted to pay them for security, then so be it.

CCM was partnering with the Secret Service, as well as local law enforcement. Jody had voluntarily piped up to be the appointed detail. She needed to prove to herself she could be around Evan with no effect, and she wanted him and her former colleagues to see she was still capable—had always been capable—of providing excellent security.

"Hey, if Wilder picks up on any of this anxiety, he'll yank you from the op. You want that?" Cosette leaned against the counter, forcing eye contact with Jody. "Do you?"

No. Nothing would come between her and the job. She wouldn't let Wilder down. He'd immediately given her sanctuary here at the plantation home turned agency and offered her a job, no questions asked. Not because he was her first cousin, but because he believed in her ability and ignored the lies that she'd been drinking on duty while safeguarding the vice president's adult son, even though the evidence had been incriminating.

"I want to accomplish the mission. And I don't want Evan Novak to emotionally affect me ever again." She finished her coffee. "I also don't want a couch therapy session later."

Cosette's dark eyes flashed, the Cajun in her making itself present in that feisty expression. "Mmm-hmm...keep telling yourself that. It's happening."

A knock on the door saved her a friendly argument. "Come in." Wilder opened the door, looming in the doorway. Suit. Tie. "You clean up nice, cuz," Jody said.

He flicked his gaze to Cosette. "Y'all ready to rock and roll? Lipstick perfect?" He glanced at Jody. "Gun secure?"

Cosette was coming today? It better not be as Jody's babysitter; like she'd have an emotional meltdown in public. As if reading her thoughts, Cosette laid a hand on Jody's. "I'll be in the camera room, watching people and doing threat assessments." As a body-language and criminal-behavior expert, if someone was twitchy in the crowd and up to no good, Cosette would spot them.

"Okay, let's go." Jody grabbed a pack of mints, tucked them in her pocket and breezed past Wilder, but he caught her arm, the playfulness in his eyes dimming. "*Are* you ready?" he asked with a softer tone.

What he meant was if she was ready to see Evan. "Yes."

"Then put your A-game face on." He released his brotherly grip and she marched outside the agency. The rest of the team, Beckett Marsh and Shepherd Lightman, were waiting by the black Suburban. Dark sunglasses hid their eyes, but she felt their stares. She might simply be paranoid. Maybe it was the tense political climate these days. Things could become dangerous. Fast. Jody's gut turned.

At the convention center, police were already in place. They strode toward the conference room. Cosette tapped her shoulder. "You left this on the counter." She handed her the small jar of vapor rub. She never left home without it—not with her genetic condition, hyperosmia, which heightened her olfactory senses. The vapor rub helped push out the overwhelming amount of smells that most people never noticed or couldn't detect.

Leaving it at home affirmed she was distracted. The expression on Cosette's face let Jody know she'd thought the same thing.

"I'm fine." Time to pull it together.

Wilder opened the door and inside sat a half-dozen agents. Evan Novak stood front and center. Jody's belly corkscrewed. Clean-cut, hazelnut-colored hair. Straight nose. Clear blue, hooded eyes and a smile that said he was old money, spoiled and full of mischief, but that wasn't true. At least the first two.

Introductions were made, but Jody refrained from shaking Evan's powerful hand. Besides, he didn't offer. Wilder gave him a cool stare and then proceeded with the security parameters and details as well as the lineup of events. After about forty-five minutes of discussion, Jody headed to the coffee bar in the conference room.

She smelled Evan approach, his wonderful scent stamped into her memory. Cinnamon and citrus. Rain and hypoallergenic, scent-free laundry detergent—which had a subtle smell. Why would he still use that now that they weren't together? Habit or as a courtesy for her? Having a highly increased sense of smell was a blessing and a plague. It sometimes brought on migraines and severe nausea. Right now, it helped brace herself for the encounter. She bristled.

"No sneaking up on you, is there?" he asked. "You cut your hair."

She inhaled deeply and turned.

His eyes roamed over her hair and trailed to her face, as if he was checking to see if it matched his memory of her. "I like it." He reached out like he was going to touch her freshly cut bob but refrained at the last second. Wise choice. She'd hate to put his behind on the ground for his colleagues to see. "I want to talk to you after the rally, if that's okay."

"About what?" She worked to remain calm. As if she didn't care, as if she wasn't still in excruciating pain over what he'd done—more like what he hadn't done. When she'd come out of that hotel room carrying his empty booze bottles to protect him, she never expected journalists to be in the hallway, but security had been breached because Evan had mixed playing hard with working hard and, for the first time since she'd known him, compromised the job.

Her picture had been plastered all over news media sites and TV. Evan was supposed to stand up for her, but in the end he hadn't. Probably because he'd been angry when she'd threatened to leave him if he ever pulled a stunt like drinking on the job again. But that night he'd crossed a line and knew it. They'd fought and she had charged from the room with the bottles in hand. Jody never should have covered for him, but the simple fact was, she'd loved him. And she'd wanted to help him. Evan hadn't made mistakes like that before. Threatening to leave him would have kept him in line. Or so she thought. They'd never know now.

He'd let her go down drowning. If she kept mulling it over now, she'd never get the job done today.

"I think you know," he said, his soft tone hypnotizing her. He'd always had that kind of power. "Can we?"

She swallowed.

"You're hesitating. That's a no." He leaned down to peer into her eyes. "But we need to talk. At some point."

Ugh. This man still knew her like he knew binary codes. And he knew those well. But he wouldn't pass for the typical computer-geek stereotype that was represented in TV shows and movies. "Let's just get through the day." She bypassed him, her hand shaking.

Wilder stood at the helm. "If you're not a praying person, you're welcome to step out, but at CCM we pray before we do a job." No one left the room. He nodded once and team member Beckett Marsh stepped up. Wilder always called for the prayer, but he'd never once led it. Beckett prayed for their protection, wisdom and safety for all.

The convention center was already filling up, the crowd's conversation creating a dull roar. The backdrop bled red, white and blue. Chairs flanked the podium, which protruded front and center from the pristine stage. Excitement, concessions, sweat and hundreds of perfumes and colognes hung in the air, sending Jody's senses into overload. She dabbed vapor rub above her upper lip to help her nose stay focused and tamp down on a possible headache.

A local official introduced Senator Townes. "Ready, Mr. Wiseman?" she asked her client.

"Of course."

Evan nodded and they escorted their details up the stairs to the stage. Atlanta PD worked crowd control at the stage floor. Jody adjusted her earpiece and mic as she scanned the seats padded with supporters and protestors, all holding signs that contradicted one another.

Static crackled over the earpiece, then Wilder spoke. "We've got a situation outside with protesters. Keep eyes on the wolf and his cub."

"Roger that," team member Shepherd Lightman said through the line. He was at the stage floor with law enforcement, observing with hawk-like skill.

Jody inched closer to Mr. Wiseman —the cub—as Evan and the two agents with him went on high alert. The senator continued his passionate speech on the Second Amendment, oblivious that something sinister might be going down outside.

Her phone buzzed in her back pocket. She snatched it. Wilder.

Need you outside. East entrance.

The situation must be escalating. Waiting a beat for her position to be manned, she scanned

the crowd, that ominous feeling from earlier raising hairs on her neck. No one came, but Wilder
needed her. Shepherd caught her eye. Guess he'd
be watching Wiseman from the floor.

She slipped from her post, aware of Evan's
scowl.

Jody weaved through the back halls to the exit
doors and outside. Clearly Wilder didn't want everyone alerted to the problem or he'd have used
the mic. She was at the east entrance but only
uniformed officers covered the area. It was quiet.

No situation. No problem.

Too quiet.

She bolted for the doors inside, running down
the halls and back into the arena just in time to
hear the first pop of gunfire.

Evan Novak sprang into action, diving on top
of Senator Townes.

Another shot fired and grazed his shoulder.
He winced at the burn and hollered, "Let's go!
Clear out!"

Jody flew up the stage stairs, placing herself
in front of him, Mr. Wiseman and the senator,
gun in hand like the expert she was, but the fact
that she was using her body as their shield spun
him into a fit of anxiety—like it had when he'd
been crazy in love with her.

Where had she been anyway? Leaving like that
with no security within a foot of Mr. Wiseman?

A third shot rang out, and the crowd went even more wild, like bulls bucking and stampeding from stalls. Screams resounded over one another. People trampled each other as law enforcement worked to clear the seats and keep order.

"Are you okay, Senator?" Evan was now flanked by other agents and law enforcement.

"Egg's hatched," Wilder called through his mic.

Good. The car was at the door.

The senator nodded—in shock—and kept his head ducked as Evan and his team retreated to the exit. Another agent cleared the door first, then signaled. Evan shoved Senator Townes inside and climbed in beside him as Jody pressed Mr. Wiseman into the other side and accompanied him, her mouth forming a grim line.

"You've been shot, Agent Novak," Senator Townes said, eyes wide.

"I'm right as rain, sir. Let's get you out of here." Everyone was safe right now and that's all that mattered. When they had a moment of privacy, he'd find out why Jody left her post. That wasn't like her, and the fact that she'd left right before the shots unsettled him.

"Where are we going?" the senator asked.

"Covenant Crisis Management. The safe point we agreed on if anything went sideways," Jody said.

Like this.

Jody discreetly covered her nose. Everyone's adrenaline must be pumping out some powerful and unpleasant odors. He shaded his eyes with sunglasses, not from the sun so much as the chance to observe her unnoticed. Same golden hair, only much shorter —barely brushing her neck. A smattering of freckles across a petite nose and full lips dusted in an understated pink gloss. Tomboyish and feminine wrapped up in one exquisite package. His gut tightened and he looked away.

He had no right to think about her like this. Not anymore.

"Thank you for saving my life," the senator said.

"You're welcome." Just doing his job. Evan glanced at his shoulder and frowned. If the podium hadn't been there, he would have taken a severe hit. He slid his gaze to Jody again, this time observing her manner. Cool as a cucumber. On the outside. But her flicking at her middle fingernail gave away her anxiety, and she kept casting small glances to his shoulder. Was she concerned for him? If so, had she forgiven him for his greatest mistake?

Doubtful. If she had, she would have responded to the letter he'd written her, or called him, emailed, texted. But it had been radio silence for three years. Evan had been in a dark place long before that. The pressure of the job and all the pressures of his past he'd never dealt with had sent him spiraling into the same coping mechanism of the one person he promised himself he'd never be.

His father.

Now that he'd become a man of faith, he didn't need alcohol to help him cope or to give him the strength for another day. God was Evan's strength, but it didn't change the truth that deep down the apple didn't fall from the tree.

He wanted Jody's forgiveness desperately, but he wouldn't allow himself to dare ask for a second chance. He'd ruined the one great thing in his life, and he wouldn't risk hurting her again. History told him he probably would. How many times had Dad said he was sorry for hurting one of them or drinking *again* or any number of painful things only to turn around after a while and repeat it, ripping Mom up emotionally like a rag toy?

Evan refused to inflict that kind of pain on Jody—for the second time.

"Have you received any threatening letters, Senator?" Jody asked as the SUV drove them to CCM.

"I get them every now and again. Mostly smoke blowing." The senator pressed the heels of his hands to his eyes. "I need to call my wife. By now this is all over the news."

Strange his wife wasn't here today. "Where is she?"

"Our son was in a car accident three days ago. He's in the hospital. She didn't want to leave him." Remorse surfaced in his eyes. "Maybe I shouldn't have, either."

Evan's place wasn't to judge or advise, so he remained quiet. They made their way down the long drive fringed with ancient oaks dripping with grayish Spanish moss until the looming historic plantation home came into view. Something straight out of *Gone with the Wind*. The columned porch made a perfect square around the entire home. Tall French windows lined the front—four on the top and bottom—shuttered in black. In the summer, Evan could imagine swinging them open to let in a summer breeze. Jody would enjoy the smell of lilac. It was her favorite…or it used to be.

Several white rockers decorated the top and bottom porches.

Two more black SUVs parked in the circular drive. Wilder Flynn bounded out and stomped inside.

"That's never a good sign," Jody mumbled and climbed out, but hesitated and then turned toward Evan. "You need to see about that wound, Evan."

Evan.

He'd missed the sound of his name on her

tongue. He choked back the emotion, the regret, the loss of a future with her. "I'll be sure to do that."

The inside of the plantation home was as impressive as the outside. A magnificent split staircase garnered immediate attention as the focal point while the parlor to the right invited guests to its sleek dining table. Gray couches were placed against each wall, and the fireplace at the end of the room roared and crackled. Perfect for this January weather. Above the mantel hung a painting of a startlingly lovely woman who shared Wilder's green eyes, black hair and squared chin. The engraved plaque underneath read: In memory of Meghan Flynn. Ah, his sister who'd been murdered several years prior.

Wilder directed everyone inside the dining/conference room but laid a hand on Evan's uninjured shoulder. "Hey, Cosette will fix you up. Guest bathroom with a first-aid kit is down the hall on the left of the foyer."

He hadn't offered Jody's services to patch his graze. Evan understood Wilder's need to look after his own—his kin. "Thanks." He followed the dark-haired woman with ruby-red lips to the bathroom and let her clean his wound regardless of the awkward tension. Who knew what Jody had told her? Probably everything. Cosette finished up and tossed her latex gloves in the trash can.

"All done, Agent Novak."

"Evan."

"Agent Novak it is." Her tone was made of steel and heat. "She's my best friend."

Fair enough. He excused himself to the dining/conference room. Coffee had been served and the senator sipped a cup and answered the same questions Evan and Jody had asked in the SUV. Afterward, Cosette discreetly offered Senator Townes and Mr. Wiseman guest rooms, where they could rest and call family while the agents with Evan and the CCM team, except one who was missing, stayed in the parlor.

"I don't understand," Wilder said. "That place was surrounded. How did someone get into the convention center with a rifle and not get dinged in Security?"

Beckett took a cup of coffee from a redhead and winked. "Professional. The senator's website has a calendar of events six months in advance. He probably hid the weapon weeks ago. Walked right in today and bypassed the extra security."

They continued to speculate and discuss the events over lunch, and then the missing team member—Shepherd Lightman—made his presence known, a scowl on his face. He motioned Wilder out of the room and a few minutes later they returned, both wearing grim expressions. "Could we speak privately with our team and Agent Novak?"

Evan nodded and the other Secret Service agents slipped from the room. Wilder closed the pocket doors. "Go ahead, Shepherd. Tell him."

"Tell me what?" Evan's pulse kicked up a notch.

Shepherd folded his arms across his chest. "I did some investigating of my own. Based on the trajectory path of the bullets, the shots fired—three in all—came from a vent in the nosebleed section on the south end. Which means someone had access to the blueprints of the building or access to someone who had them. He managed to get by Security—possibly disguised as a maintenance worker or something—and he made his way into the ductwork and to the vent where he more than likely had stashed his rifle in preparation."

Evan frowned. "Why can't my colleagues hear this?"

Shepherd's jaw ticked. "Because I don't believe the senator was the target. The first shot fired caused the crowd to panic and struck low as if he missed the senator. But no one this organized and well hidden—and able to exit the scene without being detected or arrested—is going to be a bad shot."

What did this mean? "You think the first shot was to purposely cause a panic and create chaos?"

Shepherd nodded. "And to throw off law enforcement, which it has."

"But not you?" Evan asked.

"No."

Wilder stepped up. "Shepherd happens to be one of the top three snipers in the world. And he has an uncanny ability to observe things most people don't."

"I'm not questioning anyone's ability." Evan didn't doubt Wilder's team. "I just want to understand all the facts."

"The facts are," Shepherd continued, "the second shot grazed your shoulder when you dived. A moving target isn't easy...for some."

Wait...moving target? "The third shot came when we were bolting from the stage." His neck turned hot.

"Right. But you were shielded by other agents, so it wasn't easy and the shooter had to know he was pushing his limits and needed to jet."

Evan massaged the back of his neck. "Are you saying that I was the target?"

Shepherd glanced at Wilder and back to Evan. "That's exactly what I'm saying. But the shooter wanted it to appear that the target was Senator Townes. The question is why?"

Why, indeed? Evan paced near the fireplace, though his whole body was already inflamed. "Well, it's not like I don't have a fair share of enemies."

A younger man entered the room. Tall. Lanky but not out of shape. Unruly copper hair and black-framed retro glasses. "I got what you asked for." He handed a stack of papers to Wilder and looked at Evan and grinned. "Nice work."

What was he talking about? Today? Today was not nice work.

Wilder whistled. "You've been a busy man, Agent Novak." He glanced at the guy in glasses. "Nice job, Wheezer. Wheezer is our computer analyst. Meet Agent Evan Novak…a cyber genius in his own right."

"Yeah, he is." Wheezer shook Evan's hand. "I've been reading through some of your cases. You're infamous underground."

Yes, Evan was well aware, and this guy going on and on both embarrassed him and sent a surge of pride through him. Evan had always been good with technology and it had come in handy when taking down identity theft and fraud rings online. Over a dozen cracked cases to date. If he was successful with the newest cyber mission he'd been tasked to lead, he was a shoo-in for the promotion to Assistant Director of the Office of Protective Operations. He'd worked tirelessly to climb the ranks. To validate he was an honorable and worthy man. Everything Dad never was.

Guilt stabbed his chest.

Jody had been on her way up, too.

Until he'd shot her down.

She stood silent in the corner of the room, face unreadable.

"I guess we need to decide who might want you dead most," Wilder said.

"A random criminal with a vendetta would want credit for taking you out," Jody said. "He wouldn't hide it. And while the rally was advertised on the senator's website, nothing advertised that you'd be on the protection detail. So if the hit was directed at you, then someone knew exactly where you'd be today."

"You think it was someone on the inside? In my office? Why?" Anyone in the Macon field office would know he was at the rally, plus the few agents that were on the online task force he'd been leading. But Evan couldn't imagine any one of them wanting him dead.

"I don't know, but we need to figure it out," Jody said.

The only person he could fathom on the right side of the law who might want to take a shot at him was Jody herself and she had left her post. Why? "Hey, where did you go? When you left the stage?"

Jody's eyes narrowed. "Why?" The accusatory glare drilled into him. "You think I shot you? If I were going to shoot you, I'd do it at close range so you'd know exactly who it was coming from."

Evan swallowed hard. Okay, maybe she hadn't forgiven him if she'd imagined how she'd kill him. "I know you aren't the shooter. I just want to know why you left your post."

"You abandoned Mr. Wiseman?" Wilder asked.

"I didn't abandon anyone." Jody's tone was low and cool. "I was following *your* orders. I thought you wanted to keep the situation with protesters outside contained to CCM. But you weren't out there. I came back inside when the first shot rang out and hauled it back onstage."

Wilder frowned. "Jode, I never gave you any orders."

Jody snatched her phone from her blazer pocket. "Yeah. Ya did." She tapped her screen and shook her head. Her jaw dropped. "Wilder, you did. I promise…but…it's not here. All your other texts are, but not the one that told me to get outside to the east entrance."

"Because I didn't text you." He scrolled through his phone and held it up. "Nothing."

"Can I?" Evan reached for her phone and swiped through her apps. Nothing suspicious or visible to the naked eye. Jody wasn't a liar. If she said Wilder texted her, then what she saw was a text from Wilder. Or who she thought was Wilder.

He glanced at Wheezer, and the other man nodded and looked at Jody. "Sounds like someone hacked your phone."

Jody's face paled. "Why? Why not text Evan to abandon his post and take a shot at him outside? What's the point of getting me off the stage? Wiseman wasn't the target."

Evan wasn't sure. There wasn't a good reason other than it was causing turmoil and confusion right now. The insistence in her tone as she'd declared her innocence to Wilder about abandoning her station must have brought up what happened three years ago. Of course, it was never off Evan's mind. He'd wanted to go to bat for Jody. He'd told her he'd have her back, come clean that it was his fault. In the end, he'd been a coward. His weak justifications—no, excuses—had kept him from revealing the truth. If he'd lost his position with the Secret Service, he'd have nothing left. He'd have ended up like Dad.

Why would someone want to hurt or take an emotional stab at Jody? Why would someone want to kill Evan—someone with intimate knowledge of his whereabouts and maybe even his past with Jody? But no one knew that! She'd taken her dismissal and walked away without looking back. Without throwing Evan under the bus. He'd never known why. But he wanted to. Why protect him when he hadn't protected her?

He would protect her now. She'd been tossed into this whole fiasco. He'd make sure she got out. As far as knowing why they hadn't texted him? "I don't know," he said.

Wilder huffed. "What are you working on now? Could it be linked to the attack today?"

Evan's eye twitched. "Actually, I'm leading a relatively new cyber task force, but I trust every agent on the team." There was no way one of them would betray him and there was no reason any of them should.

Standing, Wilder folded his arms across his chest. "You need to tell us about this new task force, and every agent working on it. We'll need a list of people who knew you'd be at the convention center today. Colleagues, friends. Family. Because someone knew, Novak. And they tried to kill you."

TWO

Jody needed breathing room. She stepped out onto the porch, welcoming the wintry wind before she had to hear about Evan's task force. Her emotions were all over the place. Fear of seeing Evan. Irritation that she'd been attracted all over again. Depressed at how things ended the way they had. Bitterness over how he was propelling into *her* dreams when he didn't deserve them. The anger from his questioning her performance earlier had dissipated, leaving her with confusion. She'd never compromise her job.

Except the time she had for him. And it had cost her dearly.

Why would someone hack her phone and involve her? Unless she was a target, too. But no shot had been directed at her, so what was that all about?

"Hey." Beckett Marsh's wife, Aurora, walked out onto the porch and handed her a to-go cup of coffee—the good stuff from her new coffee shop in the business district downtown, Sufficient Grounds 2.0, named after her original café that had burned down when she lived in Hope, Tennessee. "Amy and I brought coffee and pastries. Of course, I think Amy just wanted to see Wheezer."

Even their computer analyst had found love.

"I met Evan." Aurora had become a good friend and Jody had confided in her about him and their past.

"I'm fine."

"So that's why you're out here alone while everyone else is inside." Aurora grinned and sipped her coffee. "I know his coming here has unearthed a million feelings, but maybe it's a chance to put the past behind you and move forward."

Jody didn't want a deep discussion about moving forward and happily-ever-afters. She didn't believe in those anymore—didn't believe in heroes who loved and died sacrificially. She'd learned that in Afghanistan when her best friend had been assaulted by someone she trusted. Someone who was supposed to be an officer and a gentleman. Turned out they were few and far between. The assault was swept under the rug, and Jody had been blacklisted and demoted when she wouldn't let it go. But it had really become clear when Evan betrayed her and her happily-ever-after died with her dreams.

Enough of this pity party, though. "Let's go inside. I have to hear about this new task force Evan's leading." Hear about how he'd moved on without a care in the world. As if nothing had happened. As if Jody never meant anything to him. If she kept up this thinking, Cosette would notice and demand an hour to process. To talk. She entered the parlor, avoiding eye contact with Evan.

Wilder crossed one leg over his knee. "Okay, Novak. Tell us about this task force because you say it's relatively new and with the timing of this shooting, I think it could be a link. Not to mention they all knew you'd be at the convention center today."

"Again, I don't think anyone on my task force is behind this. But..." Evan cleared his throat. "The operation is called Gunmetal, comprised of ATF, Homeland Security, FBI and Secret Service. We've been monitoring a dark web website called the Arsenal for a few months. It's a virtual marketplace where anyone can sell illegal guns, and it's practically impossible for law enforcement—or anyone else—to trace buyers and sellers thanks to the N-cog browser and software."

"What's that?" Jody asked.

"I use it sometimes," Wheezer said. He would know about all things dark and secret that lay way beyond the normal internet. Jody wasn't techy. At all. She could barely figure out her TV remote.

"It provides browsing and purchasing anonymity as well as anonymous emailing ability. N-cog is short for Incognito. No browsing history and it protects you from outside sources monitoring where you've been and what you've looked at, unlike when you use Google Chrome or another internet browser, which keeps a record even if you clear your browsing history. Nothing is really gone."

"Except if you use this N-cog browser. It's undetectable?" Jody asked.

"Right. And because it's an open network, anyone can download and use it for free. Voilà, everything you do on the internet is now hidden and untraceable."

"The US government created it," Wheezer said.

"With some IT experts about a decade or so ago," Evan added. "Originally it was meant for military and government so they could protect their investigations, communications and intel. Whistle-blowers use it to protect themselves, and people in Communist countries can get real news without repercussions. It has the potential to be amazing. Even for the average person who might not want to see a Facebook ad pop up with what they just looked at on Amazon thirty seconds before. This browser won't allow any traffic analysis."

"But criminals got wind of it and corrupted it."

Bad people using good things for evil gain, Jody thought. *Timeless.* "I guess you're creating an undercover sting with false usernames to take down these particular gun dealers on the Arsenal?"

Evan smiled, and something like admiration in his eyes unnerved her. "Yes. We're trying to get them and take down the Arsenal website along with its creator. He goes by @Lawman1. Ironic, isn't it? He's a pompous jerk. Taunts law enforcement openly on his online forum. But he's not invincible. He'll make a mistake. And I'll find him."

Of course he would. It would help him climb the career ladder in the Secret Service.

"I did a little background on you, Agent Novak." Wheezer had that look. He was man-crushing. "They call you the Wasp underground."

"Why?" Jody asked.

"Wasps eat spiders. Fly right into their web and snatch them," Wheezer said. He was like a puppy over Evan.

Evan shifted, as if uncomfortable with the praise. That was new. "I may have had a hand in taking down some nasties."

"Enough that there's buzz on dark web online forums discussing you and fearing you," Wheezer added. "Cool."

Okay, all this going gaga over Evan needed to be stopped. "So back to this site and task force," Jody redirected.

"Right." Evan leaned forward, elbows on his knees. "You can buy anything on the dark web from guns to fake identities. Drugs. Even people. It's a sick place to be. The Arsenal has an array of gun dealers. One particular gun dealer has caught the eye of the ATF because their biggest line of guns are ghost guns."

Wilder groaned. "Those jokers can't be traced. No serial number."

"Cop killer guns," Beckett said. "A favorite among gangbangers."

Evan licked his lips and nodded. "These particular gun dealers that supply the ghost guns use fake identities purchased from other dark websites to help them traffic the weapons across borders and throughout the US. I'd like to get them, too. If we can bust these gun sellers, we might be able to get the criminals making fake identities and the site creator. Which means we could take down the whole Arsenal website and a lot of other really bad guys."

"Can't you track the payments?" Jody asked.

"No." Evan balled his fist. "They're almost all using digital currency. Bitcoin. It doesn't show names of account holders, only a long list of letters and numbers in a public forum called a blockchain."

Jody was going cross-eyed. Evan must have noticed. "Every time a transaction is made using digital currency it shows up but not with a name of an account holder. The list grows and grows with every transaction and that long list is called a blockchain. It's made up of letters and numbers unique to the account. But never any names, and the accounts can't be linked to a physical address."

"Basically what you're saying is that these dark websites, the users and the money they're exchanging are untraceable." Jody pinched the bridge of her nose.

"In a nutshell. But someone is bound to make a mistake somewhere and we'll be waiting. In the meantime, we're working undercover to buy a major shipment of ghost guns. These guys are some of the few who do physical trades with actual cash."

"And it'll get guns off the street and out of criminals' hands." Jody tried to make sense of all this darkness. It was overwhelming. "How many are on the task force?" Time to narrow down who might have betrayed Evan.

"Eight. We're all based out of Georgia." Evan poured another cup of coffee and added a splash of cream.

Would any of them know about her past with Evan? Jody couldn't stand not knowing who had hacked her phone. She had a personal stake in this now. "I think since whoever did it wanted everyone to believe it was directed at Senator Townes, we should pretend it was. Not let anyone know that we figured out it was aimed at Evan. That way we have the upper hand while investigating."

"She's right," Wilder agreed. "The senator isn't in danger, though he doesn't know it, and while I'm not a fan of concealing that, to find whoever this wolf in sheep's clothing is, and to protect you while doing it, it's necessary."

"I don't agree," Cosette interjected. "That's a lot of fear and anxiety for a man whose son was injured in a car accident three days ago."

"And yet he's on the campaign trail," Wilder fired back.

"It may be his way of coping with tragedy, Wilder. We all deal differently." Her tone implied she was coming at him personally.

Wilder shot her a daggered look.

Evan rubbed the back of his neck. "Should we go ahead and hit the next city? He has two more rallies in the next two days, if he's willing to go. After today, he may cancel everything."

"He won't," Cosette added. "Not if he's dealing with his son's tragedy by escaping. And there's also a matter of pride. He's a Vietnam vet and a huge Second Amendment supporter. Guns won't keep him away. I strongly suggest you disclose the truth to him, though. I understand not wanting your colleagues aware at this point since you aren't sure who may be involved. But the senator and his staff should be in the loop."

"If we tell the senator and he leaks it, even by accident, then we lose our advantage," Wilder said. "For the sake of everyone's safety, this is the best plan. We have to think like soldiers here, not with *feelings*." He held Cosette's fiery gaze. "Someone who took an oath to protect people is harming them. I think the senator, being a vet, will understand one hundred percent when all is said and done. Our mission is to protect...and that's *exactly* what we're going to do." Wilder's words, tone and body language left zero room for arguing.

Jody agreed. She'd been thrown away as a bad egg when she'd been innocent, and someone on the inside now was getting away with corruption and attempted murder.

Evan stroked his chin. "Then we'll forge ahead as planned. I'll hit the trail and watch my back. It's mine they want anyway." Evan eyed each person in the room, including Jody. "Thank you all for today."

That was it? Evan was going to go rogue.

Hadn't he listened to Wilder's "we"? Someone on the inside was after him and he was going to move on like nothing had happened?

"You're not going alone." The words were out before she thought them through, and they kept on spilling. "Wilder is right. You need a second set of eyes on your back, and I'm going with you." The room grew silent. Tension mounted and she stood, swallowing the lump in her throat, barely casting a glance at Evan.

"Oh, are ya now?" Wilder asked, one eyebrow raised.

"Look, Senator Townes isn't traveling alone. You put me on protection detail for Bill Wiseman. If he plans to continue the rally tour with the senator, then there's no reason for me not to go." And to save face, he would. If not, she'd figure out something else.

"And you want to be his security detail while really being mine?" Evan asked.

"You don't have confidence in me?" Jody held his gaze, not quite able to read the emotions swirling in his eyes.

"I trust you more than anyone in this room," he murmured.

Wilder looked at Shepherd, who stood next to him. "Are you insulted? I feel a little insulted."

Shepherd smirked.

Jody wasn't sure how to respond. A tidal wave of feelings rushed over her.

"But the answer is no," Evan added.

No? If either of them had a reason to push the other away it was Jody. But she was offering herself up. Yeah, partly because she'd been thrown into this with the text message, but deep within, she couldn't let Evan be out there alone. No one would be looking out for him because no one knew he was in danger. Or from whom! It reminded her too much of Christine. If only she'd have known she'd been in trouble, had been approached in an untoward way by her commanding officer before, Jody could have protected her.

She blew through the parlor and straight out the back door toward the stable that didn't hold a single horse. Hay, earth, decomp and animal droppings flooded her senses. Reaching into her pocket, she pulled the small jar of vapor rub and smeared some under her nose.

She kicked a stall door and held in tears.

She was over shedding tears because of Evan Novak.

She was over *him*.

"Jody?" Evan's voice floated like a gentle breeze.

"What?" She spun around.

He opened his mouth to speak, but it seemed words failed him and he raked his hands through his hair and sighed. "I said no because I don't want to put you in danger."

Seriously? "You do know that this is my job. It's in my DNA, all I've ever wanted to do. Navy, police force… Secret Service." She gritted her teeth. "CCM. I've been putting my life on the line since I was eighteen. I chose it." More like it had chosen her. She may be a Gallagher, but she was also a Flynn on her mama's side. "So don't use this as some excuse to escape me. I would never let what happened between us personally or professionally interfere with the task at hand." That had to be it. Or he simply didn't want to be around her. Well, she wasn't the one who'd betrayed him.

Evan closed the distance between them, and even through the vapor rub, his scent whirled her into the past. Into fond memories. And painful.

"I don't think that. I don't want to put you in danger because I've hurt you enough, and to know that I might cause it again… I can't do that. I *won't*. I'm not saying someone can't watch my back." His soft tone was like lulling a baby, and it held regret. His eyes mirrored it. "Just can't be you."

Now he was concerned about her welfare? If she hurt or not?

"I received that text. No one else. Someone wanted to make me look like I wasn't doing my job. I can't help but think whoever it is knows a little—or a lot—about what happened in our past." She paused to hold in the quiver. "This isn't just about you anymore. It's about me. It makes sense for it to be me." Besides, she always finished what she started even if it got her in trouble. That might be as much of a weakness as a strength. "So here we are."

"Here we are," he whispered, and held her gaze. Intense. "About our past. I need to—"

"I need to not. Let's leave it where it belongs. Dead and buried. I'm going with you on this tour if Wiseman agrees to go. If not, we figure something else out. But under no circumstances will this get personal. Civil. Not even friendly. Do I make myself clear?" Her heart couldn't handle another battering. Talking about it would open up wounds that had scabbed over long ago.

A deep pain flickered across his face, and she almost apologized but held firm. "Okay, Jody. Whatever you want. I'll do whatever you want."

Why hadn't he done whatever she wanted three years ago? Tears nearly erupted and she wasn't going to allow him the show. "I—I want you to leave now."

He nodded and left her alone.

No fight.

Like he always did.

Like the CCM resident psychologist said, the senator wouldn't back down and neither did Mr. Wiseman. They'd spent the night at CCM and on Sunday, Evan had accompanied some of the team—which didn't include Jody—to church. That didn't surprise him, though. In the four years he'd dated Jody, she'd never once gone to church except on Easter and at Christmas, but that was because she said her mama guilted her into it. But she did keep a Bible in her nightstand drawer. So at some point she'd had faith.

What was surprising was Jody's reaction to seeing Evan go to church. But she didn't want to talk about their past and she wouldn't discuss what had happened in between their past and present.

Monday morning, Beckett Marsh's wife had fixed a big breakfast and then he and his team, along with Jody and Mr. Wiseman, set out for the hour-and-a-half drive to the Columbus Civic Center. Local law enforcement had been in contact with his team to coordinate safety precautions. SWAT had been called in, as well, due to the assassination attempt in Atlanta.

Evan had checked in with his Special Agent in Charge, Clive Bevin, but he kept the truth about the real target to himself. They'd been friends for over eight years, and Evan hated not divulging to him. But for now, until he knew who was trying to take him out and why, he had to rely on Jody and the team at CCM.

A notification popped up on his phone.

Morning Scripture. He'd set his phone to deliver one in the morning and afternoon to help him stay fixated on good things. Like that verse in *Philippians*. Think on things above. Plus, he didn't know a lot of verses but he wanted to. Glancing down he read the morning verse.

A man hath joy by the answer of his mouth: and a word spoken in due season, how good is it!

How true that was. *God, help me know the right words at the right time to talk to Jody.*

Another notification came to his attention. His investigative support assistant, Layla Scrivener. She was a whiz in the office and took a major load off him. She'd emailed to let him know he and his team had already been checked into the hotel so they could bypass that part and get the senator straight into his room.

Perfect.

The senator looked pasty. "Hey, it's gonna be okay. One attempt doesn't mean it will translate into another one." He was talking to himself of course. Maybe the head doctor had been right. This guy wasn't in danger, but he was carrying the stress of someone who was. Evan didn't feel good about the deception.

He sent a text to Jody.

I'm having second thoughts about withholding info from the senator.

Jody sat behind him so he couldn't see her, but his phone buzzed.

I don't like it either but when he knows it's u, he won't want u up there w/him. Can u blame him?

Evan hadn't thought about that. Senator Townes needed Evan up there. He was in charge, and while he trusted his colleagues, he trusted himself most. Probably came from years of relying on no one *but* himself. When Dad had finally walked out, Evan had gotten a job to help his mother pay bills. He'd had to be the man, the leader. She was fragile. Always had been. He'd cooked, worked, cleaned, made sure the crummy car had gas and oil changes.

And then he'd gone and become his dad with the drinking and failing the woman he'd claimed to love. How had that happened?

What was the best course of action? Let the guy freak out for a couple of days but know he was safe, or tell him and risk something happening and Evan not being close enough to protect him? Or...

"Senator, are you sure you want to go through with this rally?" Evan asked. If he could get him to back down, Evan wouldn't have to lie and feel bad about it, and he could still hide the fact that someone had targeted him and not the senator. "I strongly feel that canceling isn't a sign of weakness but precaution."

He glanced back at Jody.

"Your wife is probably sitting by your son's side worrying about you both, Senator. Maybe you need to withdraw because she needs you," Jody said. Nice touch giving the senator a way out that wasn't cowardly but family oriented. And she was right.

"We're coming up on our hotel, Agent Novak," the agent driving said.

"Circle the lot twice. Keep your eyes peeled, boys." Evan turned and Jody raised an eyebrow. She never minded being called a guy or a dude… or a boy in this case. But she was far from male. Tall, nearly 5'10". Muscular but in a sleek way. Her new haircut showcased her long, slender neck. His mouth went dry and he trained his eyes on the parking lot. Nothing seemed suspicious, but he had a bad feeling.

"Davis, Martin," he said to his colleagues, "I'm gonna do a preliminary sweep on foot with Miss Gallagher before we escort the men through the kitchen entrance." No way she would let him go without her. "Cover Senator Townes and Mr. Wiseman." Jody and Evan exited the vehicle.

This morning was slightly warmer than yesterday. The air was calm. The lot silent.

Jody walked a few feet from the SUV and scanned the parking lot, her eyes resting on the Dumpster with a wooden fence built around it. She moved toward it, slipping her sidearm out and sliding off the safety. The woman had a sniffer like a dog. It was kind of freaky and at the same time cool like a superpower, but he'd also placed many a cold rag on her brow when a migraine from overload hit or she'd thrown up from a sensitive gag reflex to the scents.

"What is it?" he whispered, and moved closer.

"I don't know. Trash, grease…and musk from deodorant but not from someone who lingered in the parking lot. It's too fresh. It's not you, not anyone with us…" She cocked her head. Her eyes widened and she hollered as the wooden gate door burst open. "Get down!"

Evan lunged and tackled Jody, toppling them behind a blue Ford Focus as a man in dark camo opened fire with an AK-47 assault rifle.

Shielding Jody, they hunkered down behind the car, then she scurried out from his shelter and fired back.

The man dodged behind the wooden door that had swung open.

A dark van screeched into the lot as more gunfire cracked their direction.

"Stay down," Evan yelled to Townes and

Wiseman in the SUV. The van gave the masked man time to dart from the Dumpster area and across the fast-food parking lot next to the hotel.

One of the agents pursued on foot, weaving through the cars.

The passenger popped off a few more rounds before the van squealed away.

"Get that plate number!" Evan screamed. He wasn't in a position to see it for himself.

Jody heaved a sigh; sweat popped on her forehead. "Why are you protecting me when you're the target?"

Evan turned, sitting with his back against the tire of the car they'd used as a shield. "Because you were a sitting duck. What would you have me do? Let you get killed to prove some kind of point?"

Jody stood. "I'm supposed to be covering you."

Evan chuckled but it lacked any humor.

"Why is that funny?"

"It's not." It wasn't. How could he explain his instinct wasn't ever for him? It was always for her. "None of this is humorous, Jo."

"Don't call me that."

His pet name for her. "It slipped out. I'm sorry." He headed for the SUV and they secured the area and escorted the men inside. The agent who was in pursuit came back with nothing. The gunman on foot got away. No one got the plates on the van.

A sniper rifle attempt in Atlanta. Sleek. Stealth. Professional.

And an AK-47 attempt now. Not thought out. More like a gang hit.

Jody ran a hand through her hair and Evan couldn't help himself. "Are you sure you're okay?" No, he hadn't asked his other agents if they were, but Jody was different. He had to see her as nothing more than a colleague. But he'd never seen her as that. He'd been mesmerized by her from the first day they'd met on duty. First it was her looks that had stunned him and then her prowess and ability.

But when he'd fallen in love with her, the risks she took affected him in a profound way. He wanted to look out for his assigned person, but he found he was always watching Jody's back, too.

She ignored him and made coffee as she talked with Mr. Wiseman. The senator sat in the hotel suite living room.

"Senator, who all knew you'd be staying at the Windermere Hotel?" Evan needed to narrow down how the shooters knew where they'd be staying.

"Just my wife and campaign manager."

One of them might have told someone, but chances were the information came from the inside. Unbelievable.

"And, after this second attempt, Agent Novak, I agree we should cancel the remaining rallies."

Evan would have to go back to the field office, be near a wolf in sheep's clothing and pretend he had no clue that one of them wanted him dead.

THREE

"So, this is my place." Evan climbed out of the SUV, Wilder and Jody with him. After the mess went down at the hotel on Monday, he'd planned to come home to Macon and back to life as usual with hopes of discovering who might have had something to do with the attacks at the convention center and the hotel. Alone. But Wilder and Jody insisted he needed backup and they were going to hole up in his house.

He wasn't thrilled about it. Not because he didn't find some comfort in knowing someone had his back, but having Jody under his roof indefinitely was a distraction. In part because he was still attracted to her and partly due to the fact that she was a walking billboard reminding him of who he truly was and what he'd done. It hurt too much.

He walked up the drive, used his phone and opened the garage.

"That's nifty," Wilder said.

Evan held up his phone. "My whole world is on this bad boy. I can adjust my thermostat, my hot tub, security cameras and the list goes on. Wrote the programs myself. So I know it's secure."

"When you figure out a way to program it to cook your dinner, let me know." Wilder chuckled and looked around the garage. Jody's face was masked in stoicism.

The house was modest in a quiet neighborhood. Three bedrooms. One bonus room upstairs. He hit a button and lights came on inside.

"Imagine someone being so lazy they can't even flip a switch. Not judging. I like it," Wilder said.

"I can run my sound system and TV with it, too," Evan added.

Jody rolled her eyes. "What time do you have to be at the office this morning?"

"Nine. Anyone hungry? That breakfast biscuit we had at five isn't sticking with me." Evan headed into his open-style kitchen. "Bagels? Toast? Strudel?"

"Can you run the toaster with your phone?" Wilder asked.

"No. But that's not a bad idea." No one seemed to want breakfast. "Let me give you the layout of the place. Wilder, why don't you take that room and Jody can have the guest room. Bathroom is on the right. My room is on the other side of the house. We can work upstairs in the bonus room."

Jody nodded and studied the house, the mantel, the end tables. Was she looking for photos of him and another woman? She wouldn't find any. He hadn't dated anyone since her. He'd been concentrating on his faith and he volunteered at his church's gymnasium; they kept it open to the public as an outreach program. He'd been mentoring a couple of younger men. And the truth was no one was Jody. But that ship had sailed, and for the better. He just needed to keep telling himself that.

"Let's get a game plan together," Jody said. "We're going to spend the day going through some of your old cyber cases that Wheezer found. People like you so much they want to kill you," she deadpanned. "Let's see if they have connections to anyone on your task force or in the Macon field office."

"Eloquently put, cuz." Wilder made a sizzling noise with his tongue and turned his attention to Evan. "What are you going to do at work, Novak?"

"Work." Evan smirked. "Briefing with my SAC and a little hacking of my own. I know it's violating my colleagues' privacy but when one of them may want me dead for some unknown reason, I have no choice but to snoop."

"Wouldn't they be using that free browser

and software to email and communicate online privately? If so, you won't find anything." Jody toyed with the handle on her roller bag.

"True. But maybe I'll catch something. People get sloppy when they feel comfortable."

By 9:15 a.m., Evan sat across from Clive Bevin, the Special Agent in Charge of the field office and his friend. He gave him the rundown of the weekend and Monday's events, leaving out once again that he was the intended target.

Clive tented his hands on the desk. Only six years older than Evan's thirty-two, he had heavy graying and twice as many lines around his eyes. "This is why I hate officials posting their campaign rally locations on their websites. But I have one question."

One? Evan had dozens.

"How did they know which hotel he was staying in?" Before Evan could offer up an answer, Clive continued. "Let's compile a list of people on his end that knew where he'd be staying, and hotel staff. Get Layla on it."

"He said he only told his wife and campaign manager."

"Run those leads down. One of them let the cat out of the bag." He left Clive's office and found Layla, giving her the assignment.

He spent the rest of the morning making it through about half of his colleagues' work emails—feeling like slime the entire time—

and coordinating a sting operation for tomorrow night. Looked like the gun dealers wanted to make a sale. He took a break and went for coffee.

"Hey, man, you wanna grab some grub before B-ball tonight? Michael's treat." Terry Pratt, who worked on the task force with him, poured a cup of sludge. He didn't go to Evan's church but he and his son, Michael, played on a men's league with him.

Evan needed to get online and do more research, but he never missed a game, so bowing out tonight might raise questions. "I'm gonna pass on dinner. Nice of him to offer. He come into a windfall? Get a raise?" Evan joked, and added more cream to his coffee.

Terry chuckled. "Hey, when your kid grows up and offers you dinner, you take him up on it. I heard about the action in Atlanta and Columbus. Glad it all shook out. Let's hope everything does with this sting tomorrow night."

"I hear ya." Could Evan be staring at a corrupt agent? It was hard to know when he couldn't figure out the motive. And Terry? He was an all-around good guy.

"Hey, boss man." Layla entered the coffee area and grinned. "You left your phone on your desk and it's been beeping for five minutes." She handed it to him. "Y'all playing some basketball tonight?"

"Yep." Evan checked his phone. Several texts

from Jody. One from his mom. One from Sam Bass. Another reason he needed to be at that game tonight. It had been two weeks since he'd heard from him. Sam traveled for work, but it still worried Evan, since Sam shared the same problem as Evan had once had. Drinking too much. But he'd texted to ask Evan if he'd be there tonight. He texted back and assured him that he would. "Sam's in tonight."

"Good. That dude's gold at the three-pointer line." Terry dumped his coffee in the trash. "This tastes burned."

Layla shook her head. "I didn't make it. Zoey did. We'll be there tonight, too, Evan. To cheer you on." She winked and jetted.

"Hey, wait, Layla!" He turned to Terry. "See you at the game." He hurried down the hall. "I need a favor."

"I'm almost done with that list you asked for earlier."

"Oh, it's not that. It's something else."

"Whatever you want." She gave him a look that might be misconstrued as flirty, but he was almost ten years older than her. He ignored it and kept it all business.

"I need you to pull all my old case files for the past two years. Anyone not in prison, or paroled, I want them on a list. See if they've been out of town lately and if so, where." The shooter could have been someone Evan once put away, but he'd have to be working with a partner on the inside for the hotel information. The senator's campaign manager checked out. It hadn't been him.

"Sure. Everything okay?" she asked.

"Yeah, just keep this on the down low, would you?"

She tucked a strand of red hair behind her ear. "Agent Novak, have I ever let you down?"

"Not that I can think of." He held up his phone. "Thanks."

"Hey, I did that solely for me. It was driving me crazy with all the buzzing and beeping." She saluted. "I'll get you what I can by the end of the day."

At the end of the day, Zoey Wyatt popped in with two manila folders. "Layla said you needed these."

"Where is she?" Evan asked, and took the files.

"Had to leave early. Didn't say. But she did say to tell you that's only about three-fourths of what you asked for. Guess I'll see you guys tonight unless you need me to do anything for you."

Evan perused the files. "Nah. See you tonight. You know, y'all don't have to feel obligated to come to these games."

"We like them and it's a great way to meet singles." Her cheeks tinged pink and she waved. Ah, so they were using Evan and Terry to find younger men. He wasn't sure if he was relieved or offended.

When he arrived at his house, he went upstairs, where Jody and Wilder had been looking at possible threats from his old cyber cases. They seemed to have made good progress. "Anyone pop?" Evan asked.

"Plenty of people hate you." Jody dropped a file and massaged the area between her neck and shoulder. If he didn't know her so well, he wouldn't have caught the teasing in her voice. But it was true. He'd shut down millions of dollars' worth of criminal rings over the past three years.

"Thanks," he quipped. He told them about the gun deal going on tomorrow night. Wilder wasn't as apprehensive about it as Jody. She wasn't keen on the idea since someone on the inside might take an opportunity to kill him. It was what it was. He had to go. He changed the subject to avoid further protesting. "I have a basketball game tonight and I can't bail. I never miss."

"Agency league?" Wilder asked.

"No." He glanced at Jody. "Church. I'm part of a volunteer program. We keep the gymnasium open to the public as an outreach. We have teams for youth, college, young adults and even seniors."

"Ah, that the team you on?" Wilder teased.

Jody didn't respond to Wilder's jab. The surprise that he was on a church league was still registering across her face.

Wilder cracked open a can of soda. "Sounds fun. Jody, go with him. Watch his back."

"Why me?"

"Because it won't look as strange having a chick in the bleachers watching him as it would a dude like me." He gave a weak fist pump in the air. "So rah-rah-ree!"

She growled. "Fine."

"It's only about two hours. We can discuss the investigation on the way over."

Hopefully, between the three of them they'd be able to piece together what was going on before another attack came. Because Evan was certain one would.

Jody's nerves surged like live wires thanks to the cover story they'd be using at the game tonight. The best story was the one closest to the truth. They were a couple who had dated previously for a long duration and were now trying to give it another go. If anyone asked questions it wasn't like they wouldn't know the answers. Four years' time garnered a heap of intimate knowledge of someone. Why hadn't it resulted in a marriage proposal instead of a disaster? Why hadn't Jody been enough for Evan? He'd claimed to love her—been the one to say it first six months into the relationship. Jody had been more guarded.

She'd seen too many men claim to be heroic and turn out to be monsters. She'd gone into the navy believing that all men were like the Flynn-Gallagher men. Honorable. Loyal. Protective. Soldiers should have an even higher standard of integrity. But she'd been introduced to a world where not all men were created equal when it came to those traits.

Evan had had so many wonderful qualities when she'd met him. All the qualities she'd wanted in a husband. She'd made mistakes she'd promised herself and God she wouldn't, but where had God been when Christine needed Him? When she needed justice? When Jody was being blacklisted, demoted and reassigned to shut her up? God had abandoned Christine. And He'd abandoned Jody. Then Evan went and did it, too. He'd promised to defend her, to be there for her and tell the truth, and in the end he'd kept silent.

Now she sat on the bleachers watching a man she knew so well and yet didn't at all. Church? He hadn't been a Christian back then. Not that he'd been against it, just indifferent. And Jody had been so angry with God for letting her down in Afghanistan that she'd never brought it up much, and really what right did she have to? She certainly hadn't been living the straight and narrow life—that hadn't gotten her anything but heartache. And yet the tug and pull of the Lord to return to Him and His loving grace was always there. She simply ignored it.

Terry Pratt went in for a layup and was blocked. She'd met Evan's colleague before the game. Old Spice and a popular floral scent from a female perfume. She'd caught it on several other women in the crowd. His son, Michael, was musk and arrogance—it gave off a clear pheromone. And a hint of secondhand cigarette smoke. The gym had her whipping out her vapor rub. Too much sweat, testosterone, rubber soles and hot dogs.

"So you're dating the Wasp?" the redhead asked, and scooted closer to Jody. Layla. Trendy floral perfume. Grape hair product. Something with an April fresh scent. She'd met her and her friend Zoey. Both worked in the field office with Evan.

"Yeah." This was painful.

"He's such a catch."

"Agreed," Zoey said. Peach. Mexican spice… cumin…acetone from a fresh polish change. "How long have y'all been dating?"

Kill me now. "Four years when we lived in Washington. Then I moved back to Atlanta to work with my family. The distance was too much and then Evan moved to Macon. We decided to try again."

"He's very dedicated to his work," Layla said. "You must be proud."

"The proudest." Excruciating.

"He's intense to work with," Zoey said. "He can be intimidating."

"I was never intimidated by him. But he is intense." Always working harder, longer, stronger. Trying to overcome his childhood and insecurities. Jody's words of affirmation and encouragement hadn't been enough.

She shifted on the bleachers as he passed the ball to Michael Pratt, who passed it to Evan's friend Sam. She'd met him briefly before the game. Sandalwood. Balsam. Garlic that hadn't quite been masked enough by mint. Sam shot from the three-pointer line.

Swish.

Everyone jumped up cheering. The red shirts had won the game. As if Evan would ever play on a losing team. He made his way to her as she stood beside the support assistants. He ignored them and grinned at her like he used to, as if he only had eyes for her. All sweat and cinnamon. Shocking her, he bent down and kissed her on the corner of her mouth, his warm lips lingering on her skin, driving her to new levels of anxiety and longing for what could never be.

"Hang tight, Jo. I'll go change." She bit down on the emotion. Pretending to date didn't give him the right to slip back into old ways. Old names. For a man who'd never loved her, he had the act down solid. Tears stung the back of her eyes.

"You better hang on to him," Layla commented. Yeah, well, she'd been cut loose with a jagged knife long ago.

Ten minutes later, Evan returned changed and smelling like soap and deodorant. "Ready?"

"Yes," she managed to say. Her emotions were dangerously near overload and plunged right over when his hand rested on her lower back as he guided her to the car and opened the door for her.

"I'm sorry. I felt your jaw tick when I kissed you, but I had to make it appear real."

Jody slid into the car. Evan came around and got in, then cranked the engine.

"I won't do it again."

No. He wouldn't. Did this have no effect on him? "I just want to get back to the case at hand."

"Good game, though, right?" he asked.

"It was that." She'd always liked basketball. "Do you trust Terry Pratt?"

"I did. I trusted everyone in my office. Now I'm barely even telling them anything. He has access to everything. But what would his endgame be?"

"Greed. Money talks, Evan. He could have tipped off the gun dealers you're trying to take down about the undercover op, or the site creator, Lawman1. Maybe both. Which gives plenty of people reason to stop you permanently. Terry surely knows how good you are and your record shows it."

Evan's jaw twitched. He clearly didn't like the fact that someone he was close to had the capabilities to betray him. Yeah, it hurt.

"He could have offered the information in exchange for digital currency. No way to trace it, and if they had it laundered, they could cash it in at a Bitcoin exchange for money. The gun dealers might even know about the sting going down tomorrow night. You could be walking into a trap."

Evan's grip on the steering wheel tightened. "Don't you think they'd have called it off?" Evan turned left. Two blocks from the house.

Jody fiddled with her seat belt. "Not if they can use the opportunity to take you out. They don't know you're onto them. As far as everyone believes, you weren't the target. The senator was. They could off you and take the cash and guns. The agency would simply think the deal went sideways."

"That's a nice thought." His sarcasm had a smile in it.

"I'm covering every base from an unbiased angle. If the gun dealers aren't the ones after you, then it has to be the site creator. He'd really want you dead for trying to take down his site, at best, or compromising it, at the very least.

Wheezer says he gets a huge commission from each sell on his site."

Evan turned onto his street. "True. He's raking in millions—maybe billions. He'd definitely want me dead and he'd have the kind of money necessary to entice an agent to turn dirty. He likely has capabilities to hack your phone, too."

But how would he know about her past with Evan? Why else hack her phone?

They pulled into the drive as Wilder strode to their Suburban. "I was about to text you. I'm starved. Going for some Chinese for us." Wilder hopped in, leaving the door open. "How was the game?"

"We won," Evan said. "Chicken-fried rice, no onion."

Wilder nodded and left. Chinese was Wilder's go-to, and they ate it often. He'd know she'd want orange chicken and a side of noodles. They entered the house and Evan used his phone to turn on the lights and get the fireplace in the living room blazing. The silence was deafening. She'd made it clear they were to share zero personal information with each other, only keeping it civil. But she had to know. "How'd you end up at church, Evan?"

He startled, but relaxed quickly and laid his phone on the counter. He perched next to her on a gunmetal bar stool at the kitchen island. "When you left—"

"When I was forced to leave."

"Yeah," he said softly. "I'd realized my worst nightmare had come true. I'd become my father. I didn't want to hurt you, Jody."

"But you did," she murmured.

"I know. I hurt me, too." He inhaled. Exhaled. "I took personal leave. Came back to Macon to visit Mama, and while I was here I went to church with her. She hadn't been going long, but it had become important to her and it was Easter, so I thought why not? That morning it was like the pastor had planned for me, you know? Spoke right to me." He laid a hand on his chest. "Right here."

Jody knew that feeling. The way a Scripture seemed to be super personal. But it had been a long time since she'd opened a Bible, let alone listened to a Scripture verse from a preacher.

"I guess it was about six months after you came back to Atlanta. I put a transfer in because I knew I needed to leave Washington for a while. Needed out of that work-hard-play-hard boys' club."

The Secret Service agents had long been known as that since back in the JFK days. Too many agents turned to drinking and partying to deal with the high demands of the job, especially protection detail. Many times their indiscretions were swept under the rug. She'd found that out the hard way, as well. If Jody was jaded, she had reason to be.

"That's when I sent you a letter..." He left it open-ended, but Jody had never read it. She'd ripped it to shreds the day it came in the mail.

Looking into his eyes now, she saw no deception. No lies. Nothing but sincerity and honesty. She saw glimpses of the man she'd fallen in love with and also a new man. A man who claimed to be a person of faith. And Jody believed that truth.

"I've found my place at First Community Church," he continued, "and I feel like I'm paying it forward by volunteering to serve as a basketball coordinator and team leader. It's the least I can do."

The way he had put his arm around the guys and prayed—the brotherly affection had moved Jody. The fact that he prayed...and Jody didn't. A stab of conviction slid between her ribs. "And that guy you introduced me to, I can tell he's special to you."

"Which one? They're all special."

"Sam."

"He's a year sober, but struggling. I want to help him continue to succeed. I see myself in him." Evan took two bottles of water from the fridge and handed one to Jody. "His father had been abusive, too, and left them when he was only nine. The weight of responsibility fell to his shoulders at a young age. I know that heaviness."

Jody knew how hard it had been for Evan growing up and being the breadwinner as a teenager.

"I'm glad you're helping him and others like him, Evan. It's…nice to see." She wasn't sure what to say. "Is Wilder back?"

Evan glanced at his phone, where his camera feed gave him access to his home. "No, why? You smell something?"

She half laughed. "Only you."

"Sorry."

"You smell good, don't be."

Evan held her gaze.

Why had she said that? "Anyway, I'd smell Chinese food a mile away and Wilder's scent is unmistakable." Spice. Spearmint. Silicone—he cleaned his guns too often. "I thought I heard something. Anything on the camera feed?" she asked.

He looked again. "No, but let's do a sweep. Be sure."

Jody was already up. "I'll take the front of the house and east side. You take the west and backyard." She drew her gun and slipped out the front door. She waited while her eyes adjusted to the night, then surveyed the front yard and checked behind shrubs.

A crawling sensation skittered up her spine.

She cocked her head and listened, hairs rising on the nape of her neck.

Unable to see, she smelled.

Earth. Skunk odor. Pine.

She crept to the side of the house, the air chilling her lungs before blowing back in puffy clouds from her lips. She caught a whiff of chlorine from the hot tub.

An unsettling feeling tightened in her throat.

A crash from the backyard sent her sprinting in that direction.

She spotted a blade in the hand of a hulking man shadowed in black. He had Evan pinned against the shed.

The knife came down.

Evan!

FOUR

The attacker had come out of nowhere. Strong and fast like a freight train. Evan grabbed the guy's wrist, his hand barely encircling it. Who was this guy—a WWE wrestler?

Evan's muscles vibrated as he fought to keep the blade from connecting with his flesh, but the man overpowered him and the metal sliced through his shirt and ripped open skin. The burn blazed white-hot down his arm and fueled a new jolt of adrenaline.

He raised his foot and kicked the assailant's right knee, buckling the leg and loosening his iron grasp on the hilt. He flipped the jerk around and pinned him against the shed, slamming his hand against it until the knife fell to the ground.

A shot cracked through the night, startling them both as wood splintered a hairbreadth from the attacker's ear. He head-butted Evan, sending stars dancing in front of his eyes. The assailant cursed and sprang like a deer over the privacy fence. Ignoring his watering eyes, Evan scaled the fence with Jody right behind him. They raced across a neighbor's yard and down the quiet suburban street, following the man cloaked in darkness over a side fence that led into another neighbor's backyard.

A dog barked as the man jumped the fence with ease. A light in the house flipped on. Evan and Jody doubled back and tried to cut him off around the block, but he was gone like a vapor in the wind. Nothing left but Evan and Jody, and their breath creating clouds of steam.

"How bad is it?" she asked.

Evan glanced at his shoulder. "I don't know. You nearly took his head off."

"I won't miss again." She squinted, trying to gauge the damage to his arm. "You have a first-aid kit?"

"Do Secret Service carry guns?" He heaved a sigh. "He was smooth, Jody. Fought like a trained soldier."

"I noticed that. And it brings me right back to the fact that every one of you on the task force has a military background. Did you recognize him?"

Evan shook his head as they walked down the block, the wind whistling through the bare trees. A few dogs barked and a car door slammed. "I wish I had your sniffer. If it was someone I knew I might recognize the scent. You catch anything?"

"No, not from where I was. Believe it or not, I'm not actually as gifted as a bloodhound or Australian shepherd."

Maybe not. But she was good. "Thank you, by the way. For saving my bacon."

"My job says I have to." He may not have a great smeller, but he caught a whiff of teasing in her voice.

They walked silently for a block. Jody sniffed. "Someone cooked turnip greens for dinner. Barf."

Evan chuckled. "You're a Southern girl."

"Well, greens are where I draw the line." She glanced at his shoulder again. He didn't want her to keep worrying.

"Hey, we didn't get a chance to talk about everything on the way to the game. Finish telling me what you and Wilder found while I was at the office today."

She studied his arm a moment longer, then switched gears. "Wheezer did a little extra research on the people in your task force."

"I could have done that."

"Yeah, well, better Wheezer than you seeing as some of his skills involved skirting the law." She grinned. "I know what you're thinking."

"Do ya now?" Falling into comfortable banter with Jody felt good. Right. Didn't matter they were literally an inch apart—his actions had driven a chasm between them. One he couldn't deny or change. The only thing he had the power to change was the future. He couldn't get swept up in her all over again. He'd hurt her. He'd repeat history. It was like he was doomed to be his father. *Lord, please take this burden from me. Make me a better man.* He wished God would speak audibly and tell him that he'd never make a mistake and hurt Jody again. Because that's what it would take to allow Evan to even beg for a hint of a second shot with her. "So, what am I thinking?"

"You're thinking you're better. Smarter. Could do it faster." She tucked her hands inside her jean pockets. "In most cases, that would be true. But Wheezer is good, Evan. I fear what he'd be capable of if he worked for the wrong team. So, relax and accept some help."

Jody knew him like no one else. It was hard for Evan to relinquish control. Even now, knowing that God had supreme control… Evan still fought for it.

His phone dinged. Evening Scripture.

Trust in the Lord with all thine heart; and lean not unto thine own understanding. In all thy ways acknowledge Him, and He shall direct thy paths. Proverbs 3:5-6.

"Timely," Evan murmured.

"What's that?" Jody asked as they turned onto Evan's street.

He showed her the verse. "I have one sent to

my phone twice a day. Helps me learn new Scripture and keeps me centered."

"What's it say?"

He read it to her. "We better trust God because I have zero understanding of what is going on."

"To clue you in, you can trust God all day long, but that won't keep bad things from happening. Don't be naive."

Evan wondered if her reaction had to do with her demotion and reassignment in Afghanistan. He'd never thought about what Jody might have felt spiritually, since at the time when she confided in him, he wasn't a spiritual person. But now…he saw why she'd have doubts about trusting God. "You talking about Christine and yourself?"

Jody gazed out the window. "Christine was a good Christian woman. She loved her family, her country and life. She was never the same after what her commanding officer did to her. Never. And neither was I," she whispered. "I fought for justice for her. I believed God was on our side, and you know what we got for believing? Nada."

Evan knew she'd been angry and helpless, but he'd never understood the pain like he did now. "I'm sorry, Jody. Have you heard from Christine?"

"Once she was out, she moved to Arizona and didn't return my calls. I flew out there a year ago. But…she was a shell of who she'd been before."

Evan wasn't sure what to say or how to comfort her. Offering up a Scripture that gave him comfort would only tick her off. *God, please show her that You still care about her and can be trusted. Somehow. Some way.* His prayer wasn't eloquent or long, but he meant every word.

They entered Evan's house and Jody followed him to the bathroom, inspecting the wound. "Well, it could be worse. I don't think it needs stitches."

Evan retrieved the first-aid kit from underneath the sink. "I got this."

"It's okay. I can do it." She pointed to his shirt.

He hesitated, caught her gaze and held it.

One beat.

Two.

She blinked.

The air stirred thick and warm.

He swallowed and winced as he flexed his arm to shrug out of the long sleeve so his wound would be exposed for treatment. She rolled up the sleeve of the T-shirt he had on underneath.

The only sound in the bathroom came from their shallow breathing and the slow rip of the antiseptic packet.

"This is gonna sting," she whispered, her breath tickling the skin on his shoulder. She patted gently, and the cool but sharp burn sucked his breath away. "Sorry."

He tried to focus on the bathroom wall, but his

rebellious eyes continued to slip. He stared at her silky hair, her sharp jawline that portrayed the strong, confident woman Jody was. He examined every inch of her face as she carefully studied his wound and continued to clean the blood and dirt away. Her cheeks turned a soft shade of pink. She was feeling his stare. Evan ought to give her the relief of turning away.

He couldn't.

Her touch was undoing him. Soft. Meticulous. Slender fingers applying antibiotic ointment. Careful. Gentle. "Jody?"

"Evan, don't." She slid her gaze to his. "This isn't easy for me."

"You think it's easy for me?" He cocked his head, awaiting her answer. It would be honest even if it came with brutality. That was Jody.

"I think everything comes easy to you, Evan."

"You know that's not true," he murmured. But to her it probably felt true. Even if she did know his rough upbringing and how hard he fought to overcome it. He'd joined the marines when he was eighteen. Soldiers were respected, honored. Everything Evan ever wanted to be. But Jody had been indirectly hurt by soldiers, including him. She'd lost so much. And Evan? He'd sailed on through with flying colors. So, yeah, it appeared everything came easy.

She shrugged, licked her lower lip and tossed the used antiseptic wipe and paper in the trash.

"I'm sorry for the people who hurt you before me. And I'm most sorry about how much I hurt you."

"I said I didn't want to talk about our past." Her velvety gaze turned to steel. "Respect that, please."

He nodded. She was right. He was pushing. The overwhelming sense of loss swept over him. If only they could go back to when it had been good between them. When he was her whole world and she was his. When they'd loved each other.

"I will. I'm sorry."

So many regrets.

He couldn't recapture the past.

There was no future.

"Hey!" Wilder's voice came from the living room. "I bring sustenance, people."

Jody cleared her throat. "Cold Chinese is gross." She left him alone in the bathroom. Just him and his wounds. Physical and emotional. When he finally gathered some composure and came out to join them, they were upstairs and half into their meal.

Wilder spoke through a mouthful of lo mein. "You good now? Jode told me what went down while I was gone."

The knife wound didn't hurt nearly as much as the dagger Jody had plunged into his heart. No—he'd done that stabbing all on his own. "I'm fine." He grabbed his paper carton of dinner and a pair of chopsticks, but his appetite was gone. "Jody told me y'all did a thorough search into the men on my task force."

"We did," Wilder said. "Nothing hinky, but that doesn't mean anything, and Wheezer is still doing some digging."

Evan forced a bite of chicken-fried rice.

"You didn't recognize the build or mannerisms of the guy tonight?" Wilder asked.

Evan shook his head.

"Jode, you think you could sniff him out if you went into the office with Evan?"

Jody rolled her eyes and plunked her box of orange chicken on the coffee table. "Sure, just slap a leash around my neck and call *'find.'* I'll be right on it."

Wilder smirked. "Soo…no?"

She answered by sipping her sweet tea and crunching into the ice.

"No one in my office is that massive. A couple of guys in the ATF that work on my task force are, but I doubt it was either of them." Evan pointed to the stack of files and the spreadsheet Layla had made for him. He explained what it was and that he still had more coming. "Any one of those people could have come after me. But, after tonight, I'm going to have Layla narrow them down to only those with a military background." Someone had gotten onto his property undetected. Granted, Evan wasn't watching the camera feed 24/7, but still. That took skill.

Jody stood and studied the whiteboard they'd put together while Evan was at work earlier. "Someone has a vendetta or someone wants to shut you down on this online investigation—a person who is scared. They know your skill and ability."

"That could be the Arsenal site creator, gun sellers or even one of the customers that uses that site. Whoever it is has to know that I'm running an undercover task force in the first place." Evan pointed a chopstick in the air. "And that means we have a corrupt agent feeding information to one of these people. But would a traitorous agent personally come after me? What if I exposed him? I'd think he'd hire someone to do it. Keep himself hidden—safe."

Jody nodded. "I agree. Why hide the fact that you're the actual target if they didn't care if they were found out? I think they got someone else to come after you tonight. An agent wouldn't risk getting caught."

"Any one of the guys in my office and task force would have access to my home address. He'd know exactly where to send someone."

"I don't think you should go through with the gun sting tomorrow night, Evan. Like Wilder said, if he ratted you out to the gun dealers, then who is going to watch your back?"

Evan couldn't back down. This attack on him might have nothing to do with the gun dealers, and if not, then this was his chance to take them down. "I guess you and Wilder are." He hated even saying it. Putting Jody in harm's way wasn't something he was thrilled about. It was hard enough already. But she was fully capable, and what choice did he have?

"I guess so," she said, and Wilder agreed.

Now to get through it and stay alive.

Jody stirred in the guest bed. Sleep refused to come. Reaching for her cell phone, she checked the time. Almost one in the morning. Jody hated the idea of Evan walking into that sting. There were a million things that could go wrong. Evan dying was the worst. No matter what he'd done to her, she didn't want to see his life endangered.

But walking into dirty agents and gun dealers who might want him dead was a Molotov cocktail waiting to be lit. If only that was all that had her restless.

The intimacy in the bathroom earlier when she'd cleaned and doctored a wound for Evan had affected her profoundly. His nearness. The smell of longing and hope that emanated from his skin confused and frightened her.

She shouldn't be having such powerful feelings—not for a man who wouldn't marry her. When she'd turned her back on God—no, when

He'd turned His back on her—she'd really disappointed her family with some of her choices. Mama hadn't said much, but Daddy had been overly vocal with his strong opinion on their living arrangements and not buying milk when the cow was free. But she hadn't listened. Not when she was in love with Evan and refusing to heed the Word of God. Looking back, it seemed Daddy was right. Evan had strung her along. She sorely regretted living with him. Regretted so much. And even with all the regrets and pain, she still felt an ember of longing buried deep in her bones.

The whole house smelled like Evan. Even the guest room sheets with their subtle scent-free detergent. He was everywhere. In everything. Fogging up her brain. She swung her feet over the edge of the bed and slipped on a pair of socks and shoes, then tossed a sweatshirt over her head and tiptoed from the room. She needed the blast of cold air to chase away his scent.

The lamp in the living room cast shadows on the hardwood floor. The refrigerator hummed and the heat kicked on. She stepped outside into the bitter wind. Harsh. Unforgiving.

Like herself? The real reason she couldn't talk about the past was she was scared Evan might sweet-talk her into forgiving him. If she kept having these crazy feelings, moments of weakness where she missed him, he might be able to crack through the walls she'd built. Because she didn't want to forgive him. She didn't want him to think that what he'd done was okay. All she'd ever dreamed was to follow in Granddaddy Flynn's footsteps and make him proud.

Evan didn't deserve forgiveness.

Even if she knew it was the right thing to do as a Christian. But protecting Christine and Jody would have been the right thing to do, too. And yet where was God?

He was supposed to be her strong tower. Her shield. Her fortress. Her very present help in times of trouble.

So where were You, God? Where were You in my time of trouble? When I was slandered and persecuted? Where were You when I was falling apart and losing it all? Where. Were. You?

Wiping a tear with her shirtsleeve, she quietly closed the French doors leading to the deck. Winter. Wood smoke. Chlorine. She eased to the hot tub, turned it on and sat on the edge, slipping her shoes and socks off, then rolling up her flannel pajama bottoms and plunging her feet and calves into the foaming water. Steam rose and she closed her eyes.

She didn't have to forgive him to guard him. It coursed through her DNA. She'd been a protector as long as she could remember. How many times had she fought off bullies from her younger brother, Locke? Even though he'd deserved the pounding. She'd taken many a spanking on his behalf to save him from a trip to the woodshed with Daddy. She couldn't help it. When she loved, she loved loyally.

Including Evan. She'd protected him to the bitter end. Loved him loyally even when she'd had the chance to throw him under the bus with the truth. He'd been drinking too much on duty. He'd allowed the hotel security breach. But it wouldn't have mattered. They'd have rallied around Evan. It would have been his word against hers. She would have lost either way.

Dipping her hand into the bubbling water, she stirred it.

A scent on the wind arrested her attention.

The smoky scent of a cigar. Did Evan still smoke them? She hadn't seen evidence or smelled them on his clothing, skin or furniture.

Woodsy. Hint of black pepper from a seductive cologne.

Not Evan.

She turned in time for gloved hands to wrap around her throat. Meaty. Strong. The hulk who had attacked Evan earlier had returned to finish the job and had gotten Jody, instead.

Jody clasped his hands, trying to pry off the iron grip. He shoved her into the hot tub and under the swirling water.

She grabbed his forearms and fastened her feet to the side of the hot tub, using her legs and arms to drag him in with her. He tumbled in, allowing her a moment's relief. She surfaced and sucked in precious air, though it burned like ice in her lungs.

He slammed her under again.

Jody couldn't panic. She had to think. Clearly.

She used her bare foot to inch up his leg until she found the right spot and kicked his groin. He howled and she rose from the drowning waters, gulping for air. "Evan! Wilder!"

Wilder would never hear her up in the bonus room where he'd crashed, but Evan might, though the master bedroom was in the front of the house.

The man lunged. She reared back and smashed her fist into his nose, hearing the crack of bone. Her sweatshirt and pants weighted her down as she tried to climb from the waters. She was inches from freedom when a hand ripped her hair, lighting a fire into her scalp. He hurled heinous curses at her and about her. "You're going to rue that."

Fear exploded through her veins.

She sucked in a breath right before he drove her under the water with vengeful power, anchoring her to the bottom of the hot tub.

This couldn't be the end.

Not like this. She would go down fighting to her last breath.

Clawing at his hands and kicking wildly, she fought. Thoughts of Christine and hands that held her down fueled Jody. Using that pent-up anger, she dug something deep from within and found new strength. She grabbed his pinky and bent it until the bone snapped and he released her.

Shooting from the water, eyes burning, adrenaline racing at Mach speed through her blood, Jody inhaled precious oxygen and ducked as the brawny fist came for her.

More vicious curses were slung.

Hair hung in her eyes, putting her at a disadvantage.

"Evan! Evan!" she croaked, lungs on fire.

The attacker lunged and she dived across the hot tub, her knee nailing the hard acrylic outer lip and her ribs bashing against the side. She clawed her way out onto the deck, the attacker on her six like an impenetrable force.

Fight or flight.

Winded and wounded, she stood her ground. She would not let another person silence her. She would not run.

Fight.

Panting…coughing…she raised her fists into boxing position; her arms felt like heavy limbs. "You…have messed…with…the wrong… woman." Chest heaving, she braced herself.

The man towered over her and chuckled, low and menacing as he drew a serrated bowie knife from the sheath at his side. "I'm gonna take both your eyes. One for each bone you broke."

She believed he would do exactly that, given the chance. She tightened her fists, clenched her jaw. Exhausted, weighted down by sopping wet clothing, she blew a matted chunk of wet hair from her eyes. He slashed toward her and she moved to the right, bobbing and weaving the knife as he toyed with her.

This man was skilled with the weapon.

She'd been expertly trained, too. The navy. By her father, and Wilder, who'd been a SEAL.

But he outweighed her by two hundred pounds easy, and she couldn't deny the fear that sent her pulse into the speed of light. "Evan!" she screamed with all she had, and the attacker charged her.

She grabbed a deck chair and swung it full force, knocking him off balance as she ran for the house. She hurdled the lounge chairs, but he crashed onto her, ramming her to the deck floor, splinters burning as they jutted into her palms and fingers. Her chin scraped against the wood.

Were Evan and Wilder deaf? Knocked out? Dead?

"Evan! Wilder!"

"This is gonna be fun," he said, and rolled her onto her back. "Do you know how much money you've cost me?"

Money? She spit into his eyes as he grabbed her wrists with one hand, pinning her down.

Bringing her knee up, she got him in the groin again. He loosened his grip and she scrambled out from under him.

"Jody!" Evan. Oh, sweet Evan!

He raced across the deck, gun in hand. "Freeze," he yelled.

The hulk in black glanced at Evan's gun, then jumped across the hot tub and sprinted across the backyard. Evan didn't shoot—not with his neighbor's home so close—or pursue. He slid to his knees, brushed back the mass of hair from Jody's face and cradled her cheeks. He tenderly touched the scrapes on her chin.

"I hollered for you."

He pulled her against his chest.

"I'm so sorry. I didn't hear you earlier. I woke up and happened to check the cameras on my phone. They'd been blacked out. I went to your room and saw you were gone. I heard your last scream." She felt his heart beat at a wild pace. "Are you hurt anywhere else?"

She broke away and let out a relieved sigh. "I'm good."

"You give him a run for his money? If I know you, you did."

"I broke a couple of bones." She couldn't help but smile. "I would have lost in the end, I think." She laid her head against his chest again, the sweetness and familiarity bringing solace. "Evan…"

"Yeah," he murmured.

"I think you're in bigger trouble than we thought."

Evan frowned. "What do you mean?"

Standing and shivering, she wrapped her arms around her middle. "I think someone put a hit out on you."

FIVE

Evan couldn't get past the fact that Jody was probably right. The way the attacks went down— all separate MOs. The attacker from last night had spoken to Jody. Told her she'd cost him money. What other explanation was there? He must have been getting a boatload if he was willing to risk coming back. This guy knew his address. Had the ability to slip onto the property undetected and disable the physical cameras. Someone on the inside must have fueled this. If there was more than one hit man, how many more would come? And who had placed the bounty on Evan's head?

Two hours from now the sting operation would go down. Wilder and Jody had tried to talk him out of going, but he couldn't back down. Not now. So here they were at a junkyard outside the city limits so Wilder and Jody could get into place before his task force arrived.

That morning, Evan had gone into work as

if he hadn't been attacked last night, as if Jody hadn't almost been murdered in his backyard. Wheezer was combing the dark web online forums with keywords like *Wasp* and *Novak* to see if he could find a discussion about Evan that might lead to a dark web hit site. Most of them were scams, but not all, and placing a hit on the dark web anonymously would make the most sense. What scared him more than his own life at risk was the fact that Jody had been dragged into it.

He glanced at her as she and Wilder discussed perimeters. Her chin had a small scrape and her hands had been dinged up pretty good. But through the fear, he swelled with pride. The woman was unbelievable. A force to be reckoned with. She would have gone down fighting to the end. She was no coward, which was why he hadn't attempted to talk her out of being his security tonight during the sting. No way she'd back down, especially after being physically attacked. She was tenacious to a fault. Was it all out of duty? Could she possibly feel something for him? He didn't deserve it. Couldn't act on it if there was, but he wondered.

"I don't like this, once again for the ten-thousandth time," Jody said. "I don't trust this operation. We need more intel. We need to know which agent or agents have betrayed you and if these gunrunners know the truth and plan to take you and any innocent agent out. It's like we're going in blindfolded, and that's stupid."

Wilder popped a piece of spearmint gum. "I agree. But we might figure out more letting it go down tonight than not letting it. We have Evan's back."

Evan worried something might happen to Jody. "Look, we're supposed to meet at nine. Over by that pile of junk cars. It'll be me, Terry Pratt and Linn Davis from the ATF. We didn't want too many here tonight. Two more will be invisible."

"So will we." Wilder wadded the silver gum paper between his fingers. "What's the drop procedure?"

Evan toyed with the keys in the ignition. "They're bringing fifteen different models of ghost guns and we have a quarter of a million dollars."

"Wow. How did you get authorized for that much money?"

"Ghost guns are killing innocent people." Evan pocketed the keys. "We see the goods. We make the bust. Rumor has it the head of this ring will be here. He does all his own deals. But he'll have a wall of protection around him. Could be ten men. Fifteen. Who knows. We can't come with that much muscle or it will look suspicious. But our goal is to bring him and his right-hand man in alive."

Jody shook her head. "Again—"

"You don't like it." Evan waited for her to look him in the eye. "I know. But it's going to be okay. I've got you on my side." If only for a little while.

She blew a heavy breath. "Let's get into position before the other team comes to get into theirs."

Evan watched as they hauled an arsenal of weapons with them. Jody wore black cargo pants and a fitted, black long-sleeved T-shirt and black army-style jacket. She could make wearing potato sacks look good.

He waited in his SUV until his task force arrived, positioning themselves. Terry Pratt stood by Evan in the meeting place. The wind was gentle, the air cool but not freezing. Linn Davis checked his watch. "Five till nine."

Evan held the silver case of money. "They'll be here."

Terry shifted from one foot to the other and sniffed as he scanned the secluded junkyard. Piles of old cars and car parts. An empty train car. "I got a bad feeling."

Linn shoved a wad of dip in the side of his jaw. "I never have a good feeling when dealing with criminals." He glanced at his watch again. "You'd think with the money we're offering, they'd be on time. Antsy to get that dough in their pockets."

Evan had an eerie feeling himself. It slithered

across his insides, twisting them into knots. But he had Wilder and Jody in place. They waited in silence. Time stretched into eternity. Evan checked his watch. Ten after nine.

"I don't like it," Terry said. "Maybe they got spooked."

Or tipped off.

"Five more minutes and we call the contact number." Evan continued to scan the perimeter.

Five minutes passed.

"Make the call, boss man," Linn said.

A gunshot blasted, kicking up dirt at their feet and echoing across the star-spotted sky. "Take cover!" Evan hollered.

Four men appeared from behind a cluster of junked-out cars, guns blazing.

The sound of metal on metal reverberated.

Evan ducked behind an old Jeep, returning fire.

More shots came from behind them. They were being enclosed in gunfire.

Terry and Linn ducked behind a Ford F-150, covering them from the south.

"Hold your positions," Evan hollered. Two bad guys on his right went down. Could be from his task force. Could be Wilder or Jody.

Sweat slicked Evan's back and beaded around his upper lip. They had to get out of this kill zone. Terry turned. "Cover me."

Evan nodded and he and Terry weaved between cars, Evan holding his six while Linn covered a distance behind. A bullet shattered a car window. Evan dived behind the train car with Terry and Linn.

Another gun dealer dropped.

Fire ceased.

Evan breathed heavy, listening. It remained quiet. "Could be waiting. Could have run when they realized we had backup."

"Question is," Terry asked, "did they know we were law enforcement, or had they planned all along to clip us and take the cash and guns?"

"Good question," Evan replied. Or had one of his own blabbed to take Evan out? The bullets had stayed heavy on him.

A whistle sounded.

Linn turned. "That's Wallace from ATF. Coast is clear."

But was it? Evan couldn't trust anyone. Wilder and Jody wouldn't make themselves known. His phone buzzed and he checked his text. From Jody.

The coast *was* clear.

Evan and the rest of his task force met up at the SUV. Everyone shared a theory. Terry returned to the group, shaking his head. "Six dead. A couple of them were carrying IDs."

"Can't be sure they're real. Probably aren't," Evan said.

Terry handed the two wallets to Evan. "No,

probably not. But that doesn't mean we can't get a hit in the database on one or all of these aliases, and that can give us a lead to the name of the gun dealer or the people who made these identities for them."

Good point. Surely Terry wasn't a dirty agent.

"Let's call this mess in. Get some techs out here. Coroner. I'm really looking forward to all the paperwork." Terry's sarcasm garnered a chuckle from the other agents.

Linn paused. "If they knew we were busting them…how'd they find out? Nobody on the Arsenal site would have a way of tracing our usernames to our real identities."

Linn had hit the nail on the head. No one spoke—no need.

One of them had tipped off the gun dealers.

By midnight Evan, Jody and Wilder sat at the kitchen table with cups of coffee. Jody looked irritated.

"I wish we knew for sure if they'd planned to flip the deal upside down or if they'd been notified you were all agents. It'd make a big difference in our investigation."

If one of the shooters had made it out alive they could have questioned him. If only they'd caught the few that fled. Maybe the morning would bring a new lead. They'd get back online with their usernames, but they might be compromised now. Evan raked his hand through his hair. "I'm going to try to get a few hours of shut-eye. You should do the same."

At eight thirty the next morning his phone rang.

Zoey Wyatt. He rubbed the sleep from his eyes and answered through a thick fog of exhaustion. "Zoey. What's going on?"

"Hey, Evan. Look—" her voice was low "—I'm at the office. You can't come in."

"What? I plan to be there around nine. We had a late night last—"

"No, you don't understand. You're going to be arrested," she whispered frantically.

That woke him up. Evan sat straight up in bed. "What? Why?"

"It's all over the office…and the news." Zoey sounded like she might cry.

Evan turned on the TV to the national news and watched in horror. He'd been implicated in taking money in exchange for tipping off gun dealers in a sting operation. "This is ridiculous! Get me Layla." She already had files pulled and he needed her quick fingers ASAP.

"She hasn't come in yet this morning."

Evan wasn't sure he believed that. She was usually in by eight sharp. "How did this leak?"

"Anonymous tip to Channel 10, and then SAC Bevin had your emails checked after they contacted him for a statement. They found an exchange between you and the gun dealers, using your username. Five hundred grand is what they say you requested to give them the information about the setup and task force. There's an offshore bank account with your name on it, Evan. You got to get out of Dodge. Fast."

A fugitive? He could explain. Though sharing the truth now only looked like a weak attempt to get out of this mess. He snatched his laptop and checked his emails. There it was. An exchange with the gun dealers.

Anyone who knew him would know he'd never do this. And be sloppy about it? Clearly, he was being framed.

It hit him that it wouldn't matter. They'd arrest him until he could be cleared. But he couldn't aid the investigation locked up in a cell. Someone was playing a nasty game. And doing a good job of ruining his reputation, his career, his integrity.

Reality struck him. This is what had happened to Jody in Afghanistan. What he'd done to her only a few short years later.

"Thanks, Zoey. Don't call me again. I don't want to get you in trouble." He hung up and flew to the living room. Jody and Wilder stood watching the TV.

"We have to get you somewhere safe." Jody pinched the bridge of her nose. "You've escaped another attempt on your life, and I can't help but think that this is a direct response to you dodging yet another bullet. If they arrest you, then there's a much better chance that you won't escape a hit in a prison cell."

Evan sank on the couch. Jody was right. He was being boxed in to be taken down.

"Five minutes," Jody said. "That's all you have, if that. I'm not sure why they haven't already descended on the place."

"You can't harbor a fugitive."

"You let us worry about that," Wilder said.

"You're down to four minutes, Evan. Go." Jody wouldn't budge. Fire flashed in her eyes and Evan ran to his room to grab what he could.

How was he going to prove his innocence?

Jody paced in front of the fireplace at CCM. They'd gotten Evan out of his house in the nick of time, but it wouldn't be long before authorities came knocking. They'd connect the dots. Evan had been in communication with CCM for the rally and that dot would connect to Jody on a personal level, especially since they'd been seen together at the basketball game and had publicly acknowledged they were "dating."

The probability of the same person hacking her phone and Evan's emails was high. This person would have to have some knowledge of their past or it made no sense. Whoever it was had skills. The emails and the text had looked legit. They had to find a way to stop him, but running from criminals and now the law wasn't making it easy.

Which might very well be the plan of the sinister mind behind this.

Getting Evan to a safe house off the grid was imperative. They could uncover the truth if they had the time to search, which was what Evan had been doing for the past two hours. Frustration lined his brow. He must be hitting walls. But he wouldn't stop, not even to touch his food or to drink a cup of coffee. Snatching his phone, he vigorously scrolled through it.

"Evan?"

He glanced up as if he'd forgotten where he was. "Yeah?"

"Can your phone be tracked? They can get the geolocation. I even know that much." She flicked her middle nail with her thumb.

"I've encrypted it. It's safe." Thanks to consistent hand-raking, his hair poked out like he'd woken from a fitful sleep. Without an opportunity to shave, dark stubble blanketed his cheeks and chin, giving him a rugged appearance.

"You need to eat something."

"Not hungry."

"I don't care." She strode from the parlor into the kitchen and made him a turkey on rye—his favorite. Laying it in front of him with a bottle of water, she cocked a hip on the table, staring him down.

"I know that look." He took a bite. "Happy?"

"No. I'll be happy when you're safe and cleared." Evan might have let her take a fall for his mistakes, but he wasn't crooked or malicious. He wouldn't betray the agency. Just her.

"Thank you. For the sandwich."

Jody nodded and sat beside him. "What kind of person could put that much money in an off-shore account with your name on it—and over-night? It's impossible. He'd have to have your passport and banking information, not to mention financial references from your bank here to make sure you weren't doing anything illegal. I don't get it. And he'd have to actually have that kind of money to play with. All for a setup?"

Evan pushed his plate away, a half-eaten sand-wich left over. He opened the water and sipped. "I don't think it was a reaction to me slipping through his fingers a few times. I think he's an organized and prepared person. He's probably had this in the works from day one. He could have easily gotten my picture and had a pass-port made on the dark web. It's not someone on the inside—no one would have those capabili-ties and me not know it. And I don't think it's the gun dealers doing this. It's too elaborate. Which means…"

"It has to be the site creator of the Arsenal. He was told that you're trying to take down gun dealers on his site and, ultimately, his site altogether. Either he, or the dirty agent, warned the gun dealers. He wouldn't want them to get caught. It would get back to buyers and sellers and they would know that the Arsenal site had been jeopardized. They'd leave and find other sites to sell and buy from. He'd lose money. For good."

Evan closed his laptop. "Plausible and probable theory, but we need proof. Right now it looks like I'm the corrupt agent."

Wilder, Beckett and Shepherd entered the room, grim expressions on their faces. Wheezer followed and laid down his laptop. "I've been doing a search with keywords, like you asked. I have something." He turned his laptop toward Evan. "This is a dark web assassination site. You're right that most of these sites are scams. But this site is legit. It's all anonymous. And it's so deep in the dark web that you can only find it through certain online forums. It's not advertised like scam sites. It's layered with encryption, like an onion, so law enforcement is pretty much at a loss—if they even know about it."

Fear reached out and gripped Jody's lungs, squeezing them. "How does it work?"

"See for yourself." Wheezer pointed to the screen and Jody peered over Evan's shoulder, horror racing through her blood and leaving it cold.

On the screen was Evan's picture. His full

name. Address. Occupation. Age. Everything personal. Next to the information was a tiny wallet icon with a link. She pointed to it. "Click that."

"You'll wish I hadn't," Wheezer said.

Evan clicked the wallet icon and a new screen popped up.

Covering his mouth, Evan rocked back on his chair, bumping into Jody. "Someone wants me dead for two million dollars paid in digital currency. Can you confirm that the Bitcoin sitting there in the account is real?"

Wheezer nodded. "It's there. It's real. You don't have one person coming after you, Agent Novak. Or even three. The truth is you could have dozens of people trying to kill you. Any face on the street could be him or her."

Jody's bones turned to lead. "What do we do? Who put the hit out?"

Evan studied the screen. "What an arrogant piece of work." He slammed his fist on the table. Jody glanced over at the computer screen and Wheezer pointed for her.

Lawman1.

The site creator of the Arsenal that Evan was trying to take down.

So he had been clued in by a corrupt agent. How long ago? It would have taken time to get his ducks in a row in order to frame Evan.

Evan laughed, but it came out hard and bitter. "He knows we can now link the hit to him and the Arsenal. But he's so puffed up in the head he thinks we won't be able to discover his true identity. Stating his username is a slap in my face. He's saying, 'I'm so good you'll never figure it out. I'm willing to bank on it and give my online username to prove how much better I am than you.'"

Wheezer scratched his head. "Agent Novak is right. Most of these hit requests come from anonymous sources. The fact that Lawman1 made sure to let everyone know sends a strong message. And so far he's a step or two ahead of us. I'm even having a hard time hacking into the user account. Because that's the only way we're gonna stop this."

"What do you mean?" Jody asked, and glanced at Evan, who was now stalking a path up and down the floor.

"Until that money is gone or a picture of Evan's dead body appears and the money is released to the killer from Lawman1, it won't stop. I'm going to keep on working to hack into it and try to dissolve the account or retrieve the Bitcoin. No money, no motive to come for you, but it's going to take time. Days. Maybe weeks…maybe not at all."

If Wheezer couldn't crack it, who could?

Evan didn't have that kind of time. He was a fugitive now and being hunted by faceless killers.

"Let's fake his death and get the money. Stop the killers. Easy," Jody said.

Evan shook his head as he massaged his neck. "And then what? I'm still a fugitive. I go in, whoever is working on the inside knows I'm not truly dead and tells Lawman1 and the hit goes back out. This guy has the kind of money to do this over and over again."

Wilder had been quiet, that brooding look on his face. "I think the best solution at present is to let Wheezer work on hacking into the system and tracing that offshore account to find proof it came from someone other than Evan. In the meantime, you have to run. From everyone."

Evan nodded. "I'll be gone in fifteen minutes. *Alone*." He caught Wilder's eye and Wilder dipped his chin. "I don't want you arrested for aiding and abetting a fugitive. I'll find a way to keep in touch."

"I'll get you a few burner phones," Wilder said. "And some cash."

Evan excused himself and strode through the parlor.

Wilder was going to let him go alone? With everyone on the planet after him? "No," she boomed. "He needs us. He's not going by himself."

"Yes," Wilder said, "he is. It's his call. He's a trained soldier and a special agent."

"I know but…" But what? Why did the idea

of Evan out there alone—without her—send her into a frenzy?

She didn't want to go there. She was not dropping her guard. Evan was not becoming anything more than a client to her. She stormed from the room. He at least needed supplies, a place to stay. A phone and cash wasn't enough.

After she packed a few backpacks, she marched down the hall and knocked on the guest room door. When he gave permission for her to enter she stepped inside.

Lemon. Rose. Cinnamon and citrus.

Evan zipped up a duffel bag that lay on the soft yellow-and-blue quilt. "Come to say goodbye and good riddance, did you?" He turned toward the window. She caught his side view; his jaw twitched.

"If you go alone it could be good riddance forever, Evan. Please rethink this." She crossed the walnut hardwood floor, her hiking boots clunking with each step. Touching his arm, she swallowed hard. "Evan, please," she softly pleaded. "For me. If I ever meant anything to you..."

He laid his hand on hers—the one resting on his bicep. "Not fair," he murmured. His thumb rubbed a circle around hers.

It wasn't fair using herself, but part of her wanted to be enough for him to stay or let someone go with him. And part of her yearned to know if she had ever meant something to him.

Had he loved her? Or did he simply feel guilty for what happened between them?

He turned and framed her face. "Jo, if I'm caught and CCM is linked to helping me escape…once again you're stained. Because of me. I can't let that happen. The past can't be fixed or changed. I wish every day that it could. That I had a time machine. So much I'd reverse, do over, do different." He inhaled, his jaw working hard. "Let me be the man I should have been then, now. Please." He caressed her bottom lip with his thumb.

"Not fair," she managed to say.

His hand slid around her neck and up into her hair. "I really do like your hair," he whispered, and moved toward her mouth.

"Evan," she whispered back, unsure if she should let what was about to happen take place. If he kissed her, she might slip over the edge. Again. But she ached for his lips against hers. His kisses had always been skillful. Languid. Buckling her knees and blooming in her heart. Like rain on a Southern summer day.

As his mouth met hers, the window shattered in gunfire.

SIX

"Down!" Evan yanked Jody to the floor.

CCM had been breached.

A killer had discovered Evan's whereabouts. How? Inside information fueling an educated guess? Glass littered the floor, but he urged Jody to army crawl to the door. He followed, gun in hand.

"How many do you think are out there?" Jody asked.

"I don't know, but they're either pros or idiots coming onto CCM property. Do they have any clue about who lives and works here?" Outside in the hall, Evan assessed the situation. "Where are your security cameras?"

"Control office/safe room. With Wheezer."

"Let's go."

Jody led the way down the hall, downstairs and into the section of the house Wilder had remodeled into offices. Wheezer sat at his desk, gun beside him as he studied the cameras, his girlfriend huddled against him with wide eyes.

"Where's Wilder and the team?" Jody asked. "Amy, you okay?"

She nodded and held tight to Wheezer.

"Fanned out across the perimeter," Wheezer said.

Evan glanced at the state-of-the-art camera system. "How did he get onto the property without detection?"

"He's in the north woods. Shot from there."

"Wow, that's far."

"Yeah."

A pro.

Probably alone, then.

"I need to go. Now." Evan hated it. Hated leaving Jody, but to keep her safe it was the right thing to do. He wished he had the time to talk about that almost-kiss. What did it mean? Had she forgiven him? Did she…did she want to give it another try?

Did he?

Yes, but that was impossible.

"Come on." Jody tossed him a Kevlar vest and worked on securing hers. "We have to move. Fast."

"We?"

"We're going out the front doors and into the Suburban. We might make it if we move fast. If he's in the north woods. But in case he's faster…"

She patted her bulletproof vest and held up the keys. "I'll cover you."

And who would cover her? A Kevlar vest wouldn't protect against a head shot. "No way."

"Please do not play the chivalry card now. I can handle myself. I'm not the target." She drew her weapon and motioned for the door, then turned to Wheezer. "I'm taking him to Granny's house. Let Wilder know."

Wheezer nodded.

Evan followed Jody as they hurried through the house to the front door. "Go time," Jody said, and stepped out, surveying. "Clear."

Growling, Evan crouched and ran for the SUV, Jody on his six.

Gunshots fired.

Evan scrambled for the passenger door and opened it, using it as a shield. "Get in first, slide over."

He shoved Jody inside and she scrambled to the driver's side. Evan jumped in and locked the door. Another shot hit the windshield. Bulletproof. "Go, Jo!"

"Ditch that phone. I don't care how encrypted it is. Someone found you here and it may have been through that."

No way his phone was hacked or tracked. He'd written the codes himself. "This thing is impenetrable."

She peeled from the circle drive. "Now is not the time to get cocky."

Evan tossed his phone.

Another shot clipped the front bumper of the SUV. Jody laid on the gas and barreled down the long drive, nothing but dust behind them.

Had his pride endangered them? Could someone have breached his codes and tracked them with his phone? Could it have been Lawman1?

Glancing back, he groaned.

"Wheezer will find the phone and do a sweep. And before you say how great you are and how secure the phone is, remember that Wheezer is one of the best." Jody turned left.

"My whole world is on that phone. My Scripture verses!" He huffed and buckled his seat belt.

"Last I checked, Scripture was meant to be hidden in your heart not downloaded to your phone. You'll live." Her wooden tone brought a smile to his face. Yeah, he was pouting, but it irritated him that his phone might have been the key to finding him. He was once again trusting in himself and his own abilities. He wasn't perfect. He was human. Flawed.

"Well, you got your way." They were in this together. Evan was far from alone. Now he had himself to worry about—and Jody.

"That I did." She glanced at him, a smirk on that pretty face. A face he'd nearly kissed before they'd been fired on. "Don't worry, I didn't have

Shep hide in the woods and fire at us to get us on the road."

"Because you'd never do that?" He chuckled.

"Because Shepherd missing a shot—even a planned one—would tarnish his perfect record and he wouldn't stand for it."

"He's never missed a target?"

"Nope." Jody hit the interstate.

Wow. Evan glanced in the back seat that was loaded down with supplies. "You sure you didn't set that up?"

"I had planned to come talk you out of being a hero and going rogue after I packed up the Suburban, but I only tossed in the backpacks. Wilder keeps this thing loaded down with everything from bomb gear to ghillie suits." She cleared her throat. "I didn't plan on it leading to…"

"A kiss," he murmured.

"Right. I wasn't levelheaded back there. You and me…we're not gonna happen, Evan. Ever again." Her tone was calm and collected. No anger. Simple fact. "I won't lie and say that I never have some of those old feelings crop up when I look at you. I do. But that's all it is. Old feelings."

Too much between those old feelings for new ones to grow. Understood. Still hurt. But she was right. They weren't happening ever again. She was afraid he'd hurt her again. So was he.

"Where are we going?" Changing the subject was in order. "What's Granny's house? Code?"

"No. We are going to my granny's house. She willed it to Meghan. When Meghan died, Wilder took possession of it. It's near the Chattahoochee River—do *not* start singing that country song."

"You like that song." He chuckled and hummed.

"When Alan Jackson is singing. You're no Alan Jackson." She slid a mischievous look his way. "More like Harrison Ford."

He frowned. "What?" Then it dawned. "Oh. *The Fugitive.* Nice. Glad you're finding the humor in all this." He wished this was nothing more than a movie to entertain an audience for two hours.

She snickered, then sobered. "With no devices, we'll be safe at the cabin while we decide the next step and while Wheezer works to crack through to the hit site and dissolve the funds."

"You heard him. It could be weeks. You going to put your life on hold for me like that? Hole up in a cabin with me and wait it out?"

Jody turned on the radio. "I don't know, Evan. I guess we'll figure it out as we go. For now, you need to stay off the grid and safe. Stillwater State Park is the best place."

"Jody, we both know the agency, in conjunction with the FBI, will start with CCM. They'll look into all real estate holdings and check each and every one of them. We have maybe forty-eight to seventy-two hours before they realize Wilder owns a cabin *on the Chattahoochee.*" He couldn't help but sing the last words to the tune of the country song.

She rolled her eyes and remained quiet. There was no denying truth.

It was only a matter of time before the jig was up.

Neither party after them meant safety.

And now Jody was a fugitive with him. When the government swooped in on them, she'd be arrested, too. Unless they could clear both their names in three days.

"You hungry?"

"Not really, but you're going to tell me to eat anyway." He cranked up the heat. It was in the forties today.

"We'll pull over at the next exit and grab some snacks." She pointed to the back seat. "In that blue backpack, you'll find a couple of ball caps."

He reached behind and took them.

"You manage to get out with your sunglasses?"

"No. But I have my wallet and some cash." He slid the ball cap on his head and handed the other one to Jody. She always looked good in a cap.

After stopping for snacks, they hopped back on the interstate. An hour later the scenery became thick with pines as they traveled down a gravel road. Evan cracked his window. The sound of rushing waters. If he wasn't running for his life, this would be a peaceful place to relax and unwind.

"You been here before?" he asked.

"As a kid. Rafting, canoeing, fishing… There's a waterfall not too far from the cabin. It's pretty secluded."

"Sounds nice." Evan had never had those kinds of vacations. He'd never had vacations period.

They drove deep into the park and up a small hill. A log cabin with a long porch came into view. An old weathered picnic table sat kitty-corner from the house; a monstrous tire swing hung from a pine branch.

"Come on. Let's get settled." Jody tossed her ball cap and started unpacking the back seat.

At the door, she fished for the keys.

"Jo?"

"Yeah?" She didn't reprimand him for using her nickname.

"You can leave me here. Go back while you can. While it's safe for you."

She unlocked the door and toed it open, wrinkling her nose.

All he smelled was mustiness from a cabin that needed airing out.

Stepping inside, she dropped the armful of supplies on the kitchen counter. "Evan, I'm not leaving you. Don't misconstrue it, but accept it."

There was no talking her out of this. No going back. He admired her tenacity not to give up on him. She hadn't given up on him in the past, either, and it had come back to haunt her. How could this woman do it again? Stick it out with him knowing she could get into trouble—had been in trouble before, lost it all. How could he convince her to leave? It was the only way to protect her physically and emotionally.

Flashes of Mama crying in her bed over Dad solidified it. He wouldn't make Jody cry over him ever again.

"You realize the ramifications?"

"My eyes are wide-open, Evan. You're innocent. I can't turn my back on you." No accusation in her voice. Not even a harsh tone. Simply who she was. But Evan felt the conviction deep into his bones. He'd turned his back on *her*. Emotion clogged every pore in his body. He felt it burn the backs of his eyes.

"I'll bring in the rest of the supplies." It was all he could manage.

Weeks? Jody hadn't thought this through. She couldn't be on the run for weeks with Evan. The proximity alone was enough to suffocate her. The ride to Granny's cabin had given her a measure of time to resolve some issues. No more getting swept up by the past. No more getting swept up in the even more appealing man that Evan was now.

She was doing her duty. Making sure he stayed

alive. Hoping he could be exonerated. An opportunity she'd never had. But did she need to go to this much trouble? And that moment when his lips touched hers—it would have become much more intimate than a peck had the gunshots not ensued. What was going on?

Her heart tried to pipe up, but she shut it down. She did not care about Evan.

Except…she did. Cosette would have some kind of psychological term for her. Wilder would call her a moron. But it was what it was. She cared.

But she couldn't. Not in a personal kind of way.

Reaching into her pocket, she pulled out nothing but lint and a gum wrapper.

"You looking for this?" Evan held up her small jar of vapor rub. "You left it on the desk in the camera room. I grabbed it on our way out. How bad is it?"

Her fingers brushed his as she accepted the jar, then she opened it and dabbed it under her nose. "We need to open a window. Critters have died in here and there's some mildew. Metallic smell like rusted pipes. Stagnant water."

"I smell a musty old cabin."

"I envy you that." She wrinkled her nose as Evan opened a window, the biting January wind rushing in. "Wood smoke. I've always loved that smell. Reminds me of my dad." He'd passed away five years ago. Evan had been there at the funeral with her, holding her hand and comforting her.

"I envy you good memories." Evan would have no fond ones of his father. He crossed into the small kitchen that opened up to the cozy living room. Opening the fridge, he frowned. "Well, we have water and water. Oh, and water."

She snickered. "We'll have to run into town for some groceries. It's a small place. But we shouldn't go together. I don't want someone seeing your face and calling a tip line or something, and I'm sure by now there's a tip line."

Jody grabbed a few backpacks and arranged them by the doors in case they needed to make a fast exit. After she finished and did a walk of the property, she came inside to a fire blazing in the fireplace. Perfect.

Coffee. Wood smoke. The smells covered, if only a little, the other smells that had hit her like a semi truck. "I found caffeine," Evan said. "It's not a fancy brand but it's hot, black and I made it strong."

Also perfect. She crossed to the old fireplace. She'd sat on this brick hearth many times. Wilder had jumped off pretending to be a superhero and had to go to the ER for stitches. Jody had razzed him relentlessly about how un-superhero-like he was and she'd taken a few Wilder Flynn poundings for it.

Perching close to the fire, she held out her hands for warmth as Evan brought her a cup of coffee. She thanked him and sipped.

He sat next to her, cinnamon and citrus. Fear... that was a first. She didn't care what science said, she could smell fear. Excitement. Anxiety. And right now she smelled fear. "What's the matter?"

Evan slid his gaze from the fire to her face. "Nothing, why?"

"Evan, I smell it. Are you nervous someone is going to find us here?"

Smirking, he set his coffee cup on the hearth. "Authorities will. At some point. I'm trying to run down in my head who might be apprising Lawman1. I have no way to hack into that offshore account to uncover the truth. I have no phone."

"Bible's in the nightstand drawer in the master bedroom. Why don't you take that room and you can read all the Scripture you want." The fire blazed, cracked and popped. A tug of conviction came that she should be reading God's word. Trusting Him. She wasn't sure she could after all the pain she'd endured.

"Remember that time we went to Colorado in February?" Evan asked.

Jody sipped the strong, bitter brew. "The lodge in Telluride?"

The vice president's son loved to ski, and she and Evan went wherever Talbert "Tal" Derringer IV went. That guy was hard to keep up with. Constantly kept them in a state of anxiety. He was a ladies' man at twenty-three and he'd hit on Jody more than once. Evan had threatened to pop him upside the head for it, but Jody had reminded Evan that wasn't really protecting him. Tal knew it, too. Arrogant little ferret. But that wasn't what Evan was referring to. He was reminded of the seclusion. The lodge. The fire. Sipping hot cocoa. Well, this cabin and this situation—it wasn't romantic. Wasn't anything like that.

"You still ski?" he asked.

"No. No time." She loved it, though. White slopes. Crisp. Icy. Fast and furious. "You know after I left protection detail, Tal called me a few times to 'get together.'"

Evan's eyes showed surprise. "That guy is a piece of work. I knew he was totally into you and hated me."

Jody laughed. "He wanted to know if we had a chance since you were out of the picture and I wasn't assigned to him anymore. Couldn't care less about what had gone down."

"I hope you told him never in a million years." Evan snorted.

"In a roundabout way. I think he thought I'd be thrilled to date a younger man who was as wealthy and powerful as himself. I hope it didn't dent his fender for long."

"I doubt he ever recovered." His grin was sad.

"Anyway, I never liked him. But I'd have taken a bullet for the punk."

That was the job. Didn't have to love everyone, but you did have to promise to lay your life down for them. "I think he watched *The Bodyguard* one too many times."

"You're no Kevin Costner."

She laughed again.

"I found Scrabble and some Uno cards in a cabinet while you were outside charting getaway plans." His boyish grin did a loopty-loop in her stomach. "I didn't see a TV, though."

"No, this place is meant for good old-fashioned family fun." Now it was a safe house. "I guess we need to run into town now."

"Do they have a public library?" Evan asked, and drained his cup.

"I think so. Why?"

"I'd like to use the computer. Don't worry, I'll be cautious."

Jody stood. "Evan, you have to trust someone other than yourself at some point."

"I know. I do. I just…"

"Trust yourself more. Maybe you need that Scripture about trusting in the Lord again."

"I ditched my phone." Evan's voice was teasing, but it held some truth. "I have nothing."

Her dad used to say that's how God liked it. Then all they had to rely on was Him. That's how she felt. Stripped bare. Nothing left. But instead of relying on God, she'd done the opposite. She hadn't invited Him into her pitiful circumstances.

It is better to trust in the LORD than to put confidence in man.

The Scripture gripped her soul. She hadn't invited God in or run to Him when she'd struggled for justice in Afghanistan. No, she'd left the military and had run straight to Evan. Trusted in a man who wasn't even a believer, and that trust and refuge had crumbled.

She glanced at Evan. Could she truly blame him for all the mess in her life? No. She had a lot of blame to carry, too. Evan wanted her forgiveness, but she hadn't even forgiven herself for her sins.

"Let's go."

"To the library?"

"Whatever you want, Evan. I'm picking my battles and if you say it's safe, I guess I'll trust you." For safety's sake only. She rummaged through her backpack and retrieved a burner phone. "By now, Wilder knows we're here. I'm going to call and see if they found the shooter."

On the way Jody called. Wilder hadn't found anything but shoe treads. Beckett had tracked them to the back side of the woods and road. The shooter must have parked a car or hopped a ride. After the road, the trail turned cold. Every news channel had the banner running on a constant loop about Evan Novak, the fugitive, and a tip line had been set up. Then came another interesting fact. Terry Pratt had shown up thirty minutes after the shooter breached CCM.

"What did you tell him?" Jody asked.

Wilder huffed. "Nothing. I said I didn't know where he was and that was the truth at the time. Wheezer told me after he left that you'd taken Evan to the cabin."

"Did you get a vibe from Terry?" Jody asked.

Cosette's voice filtered through the line. "I was there. He asked all the right questions an agent would, but his eyes and body language said he didn't believe that Evan was a corrupt agent or that Wilder had no knowledge of your whereabouts."

"I was telling the truth!" Wilder insisted.

"Yes, well, he didn't believe you," Cosette said.

"What did I do wrong? I didn't shift or—"

"Now is not the time," Cosette said. "I don't suspect he's your corrupt agent, Jody, but I can't say it definitively because I've seen some believable sociopaths."

But he'd shown up right after. Coincidence? If he was the bad guy, he could have used his badge to secure Evan. He'd know he was there if he'd fired shots earlier. And Terry Pratt had sniper training.

"Any news from Wheezer?"

"He's still working on hacking into the assassination site to call the hit off."

"Okay," Jody said. "We'll keep on alert."

"Or you could come home and Evan could keep running on his own, Jody." Wilder's comment wasn't a suggestion, but more of a request.

"I agree," Evan said.

"I don't. Keep us posted." She hung up. "Don't say a word."

Silence covered the van.

"Word," Evan muttered, and chuckled under his breath.

She shook her head and parked on the square. "Library is over there, I think. I'm going in this convenience store. I'll come find you when I'm done."

Evan nodded and slipped on his ball cap. "That's a plan."

"Evan…" She paused. "Please be safe."

"Always."

She watched him jog across the street and disappear into the library, then she entered the convenience store. Grabbing a small shopping cart, she combed the aisles for food to last two to three days tops. That's all they had in this location.

As she stood at the checkout to pay, a cold finger of fear walked up her spine. She glanced out the large windows in front of the store. Nothing seemed out of place. No one lurking. But the sensation of being watched wouldn't let go.

She carried her sacks to the Suburban, tossed them in and hurried across the street to the library, the eerie feeling growing stronger. Inside, she found Evan at the computer center, clacking away.

"We need to go. Now."

Evan didn't ask questions. He powered down the computer and followed her out of the library. At the car, she caught a whiff of something.

"What is it?"

She shook her head and glanced at the woman with a stroller a few feet away on the sidewalk. "Nothing. I caught her perfume and it's familiar. Floral." She shrugged off the odd sensation. "Let's get back."

Evan jumped in the passenger side and clicked his seat belt in place. Jody climbed in and cranked the engine. Paused. Something felt off.

"What is it?"

Frustration and fear balled her fist. "I don't know. That's the problem."

She was afraid they'd find out soon enough.

SEVEN

Evan helped carry in groceries and rummaged through the sacks. Pasta, lunch meat, bread... nothing fancy. Quick. Easy. Jody had never been a culinary master, but she never burned anything. The sniffer wouldn't let her. It was mostly too many smells bothering her, so she'd kept dinners simple.

Man, he missed meals with Jody. Coffee afterward and great conversation. They shared the same love for slapstick comedies and vanilla over chocolate. Jody busied herself hunting down sheets and blankets. "Jo, I'll take the couch. I'd rather be at the front of the cabin than off in a bedroom."

She entered the living area with bed linens in her arms. "Okay. You still need a pillow and a blanket." She tossed them on the couch and laid the extra sheets on the coffee table. "They're stale smelling."

He doubted he'd notice. "Want me to cook the spaghetti?"

"Yeah, and you can tell me what you did at the library." Jody rifled through a grocery bag and pulled out the contents to make a pitcher of sweet tea.

Evan had quickly encrypted the computer and checked his emails. No one would be able to track his whereabouts. "I got an email from my SAC, Clive Bevin. He said he didn't believe the evidence. Thinks I'm being framed and asked me to come in so we could uncover the truth. But then I also received an email from Layla."

Jody filled a glass measuring cup with water and put it in the microwave. "Your investigative assistant? The one that comes to your basketball games?"

Evan hid his smirk. "That's the one."

"She said you were a catch." She unpackaged four family-sized tea bags.

"What'd you say?"

"I agreed. I was undercover, ya know." She glanced at him and the corner of her mouth tipped north. "What'd she want?" The microwave beeped and she opened it, then dropped the tea bags inside the boiling water.

"It was a warning to steer clear of the field office. She said that Clive's email to me was a ruse to get me to come in and arrest me." He wasn't sure what to make of the two emails.

Jody opened the pound of sugar and searched for a measuring cup. Scooping a heap and dumping it into a plastic pitcher, she said, "Who do you believe?"

He'd been friends with Clive for years. But he had a job to do and that was bringing in Evan. He couldn't fault his SAC for that. He'd have done the same thing. "I want to believe Clive. But when you have a job to do, you do it any way you can. So maybe it is a ruse."

"How would Layla even know he sent you an email to come in?" Jody asked, and poured one more cupful of sugar into the pitcher.

"I'm sure it's the buzz around the office. If it's a ruse, then they'll know and be on the lookout. I mean why would she lie? What would be the benefit of having me stay on the run?"

Jody emptied the steeped tea into the sugar and stirred. "There isn't one. She's probably telling the truth."

"Yeah. But why would Layla get herself involved? It's not smart."

"Maybe she wants to help." Jody filled the pitcher with water, then stirred again and put the tea in the fridge.

"I don't know."

Evan retrieved a skillet from the warming drawer under the stove and dropped a pound of hamburger in it. "Seasonings?"

Jody pointed to the cabinet by the sink. He

grabbed what he needed and doused the meat with onion powder, garlic and pepper. The aroma of sizzling beef filled the kitchen. Jody sat at the table, hand propped under her chin. Was she thinking of all the times he'd cooked for her? Years' worth of meals. Was she sitting there wondering where they'd be right now if they'd gotten married? If he'd have been brave enough to ask. If he could have been guaranteed that he wouldn't turn out to be like Dad.

"Jo?"

"Hmm?"

"Are we ever gonna talk about what happened? Did nothing in that letter mean anything to you?" He'd asked for her forgiveness and bared it all to her.

She came out of her lazy gaze toward the windows and bristled. "I didn't read it."

With that, she strode from the kitchen and into the master bedroom, and quietly closed the doors. She hadn't read it? Evan couldn't blame her. He might have ignored it, too, if the tables were turned. She didn't want to talk about it. Didn't want to forgive him. What was he supposed to do with that? He'd asked for forgiveness and talked to his pastor about it. He'd been doing volunteer work at the church to make up for it—though he knew he never really could.

Shouldn't God's forgiveness be enough? If so, why did his stomach turn constantly?

He mechanically finished the spaghetti and toasted the garlic bread. He placed it all on the worn and nicked kitchen table but had a feeling Jody wasn't going to come to share a meal with him.

But he'd try.

He knocked lightly on her bedroom door. "Jody, dinner's ready." She probably already knew that with the smells. "Please come eat. With me. I won't bring up the letter." Leaning against the door, he waited. Hoped.

The knob turned with a click, and he backed up as she opened the door.

She'd been crying. It killed him to see red-rimmed eyes and a pink nose. "You hungry?" he asked, instead.

"Yeah. Smells good. Thanks." She sat at the table and placed the paper napkin in her lap.

Evan served up the food and cleared his throat. "Can I say the blessing?"

"Sure." She bowed her head and he prayed.

They ate in uncomfortable silence. Finally Evan couldn't stand it anymore. "I'm going to collect more firewood. It's going to be cold tonight." He grabbed his gun from the living room coffee table and headed outside. He needed air.

When he came back inside, Jody had already cleaned up the dinner dishes. The smell of coffee brewing filled the cabin. She was curled up on the couch. Evan stoked the fire, added more wood and poured a cup of coffee. "You want one?" he asked.

"Thanks."

He brought her a cup and sat on the other end of the couch. "I'm not going to turn myself in. In case Layla is right."

"Wise decision. I called Wheezer while you were outside. He's only cracked through three layers of encryption on the assassination site. But he'll keep at it."

Evan was impressed. "That's actually pretty fast." He sipped his coffee. "Any thoughts about where we go next?"

"We can't use friends or family. We have several thousand dollars in cash. I say we go farther south. Maybe rent a boat and hit the seas for a while."

"You know I get seasick."

"Exactly. Anyone who really knows you knows that. Buy some motion-sickness meds and suck it up." Jody cupped her mug and shivered. Evan lifted the blanket off the arm of the couch and covered her legs.

"And what about you? Are you gonna be on this boat?" Evan asked. "How long are you going to run with me, Jody? You have a life, and the longer you aid and abet, the greater the chances of you doing time."

"Let me worry about that, Evan." She closed her eyes. "I'm exhausted."

Evan leaned over and took her mug, setting it on the coffee table. Jody didn't budge and her breathing evened out. The woman could fall asleep on a dime and in any position. Her neck was going to protest later. He put his empty cup on the coffee table, then he gently picked Jody up, cradling her in his arms, the feel of her against him undoing everything he'd kept bound inside.

He carried her to the bedroom and toed the door open. She lightly stirred, a soft murmur escaping her lips. Squatting with her in his arms, he pulled the covers back and laid her on the bed. Carefully he slipped off her shoes and covered her up. She nestled into the pillow, but didn't wake.

Evan brushed the hair back from her face and wished things hadn't turned out so tragically. Biting back the temptation to kiss her while she slept, he tiptoed from the room and closed the door with a quiet click. She might be a sleeping beauty, but his kiss wouldn't waken her to love. And that, too, was a tragedy.

Leaves burned in a huge pile and Jody was only ten. She watched as the smoke billowed into the fall sky; Granddaddy Flynn stood with a water hose in hand. "Where there's smoke, there's fire, Jody-girl. You gotta be safe when messing with fire."

Her eyes popped open.

Disoriented, she glanced around. She was in the master bedroom.

And she smelled smoke.

Not leaves. The smell must have brought on a memory from her past and it manifested as a dream. She slid over the side of the bed, slipped on her shoes and followed the scent. Opening the bedroom door, a cloud of smoke smacked her senses. She covered her mouth, coughed and saw the source.

The fireplace had smoke billowing from it. Had the chimney been stopped up? She rushed to the fireplace, but the fog kept her from seeing, burned her eyes. Evan. Where was Evan?

She fanned her hand in front of her and saw his silhouette on the couch. "Evan!" She ran to him and shook him. Had he inhaled too much smoke? "Evan! Wake up! Can you hear me?" She shook him more violently and he stirred, coughed. *Thank You, God!*

First kind words she'd said to Him in a long time.

"Evan, wake up." She used his shirt and pulled it up over his mouth and nose. "The chimney is stopped up. We have to get out of here."

Evan roused and coughed again. Reality set in and he jumped to his feet, fully clothed and shoes already on. "What happened?"

Adrenaline raced through her blood, fear leaving her in a cold sweat. "We have to get out of here." She ran for the front door.

"Wait!" Evan held her back. "If the chimney's been clogged it's a trap to get us out."

"Well, we can't stay in here. We'll die for sure!"

Evan threw on a backpack and tossed one to Jody. "We don't know how many there are. We have four exit points. Surely there isn't someone stationed at each one."

Maybe. Maybe not. But what if they picked the wrong exit point? They were easy targets!

Evan peeked out the living room windows, but it was too dark to see and the smoke was too thick. He coughed and rubbed his eyes. "How did they find us?"

Jody wasn't sure, but her educated guess was Evan hadn't been as thorough in covering his tracks at the library as he'd thought. Only, that might not be true. Jody had felt watched while in the convenience store.

Where there's smoke, there's fire, Jody-girl.

Her hands shook and panic threatened to overtake her senses. She kept her shirt over her mouth and nose. A flare of orange flickered in the kitchen window. "Evan! We gotta go. Now."

"Bedroom window. We have to attempt it." Evan grabbed her as they stayed low, trying to bypass the dense cloud choking them.

Smoke clogged Jody's lungs as she gasped and

coughed, her eyes blinded by the haze and burning sensation.

Heat filled the cabin as an orange flame burst through the kitchen window and licked up the counters. They'd set the place on fire! She clutched her backpack. It wouldn't take long for it to eat up the cabin and make its way to the bedroom.

He raised the window. "I'll go first. Cover me."

No way. He was the target and going out first gave him the disadvantage. "No. I go first."

Evan growled. "Not happening. Not in this lifetime. Not ever."

His eyes darkened. Intense. He wouldn't budge; he'd stand here and burn alive before he let her go out that window first and risk a fatal wound. Anger and appreciation intertwined in her chest. They'd discuss it later. They'd both die if they stayed inside arguing.

Flames dogged the bedroom door frame.

"Fine! Go!"

Evan glanced at the flames and back to Jody. Something in his eyes… "While I've already got you mad…" He grabbed her neck, pulled her to him and kissed her hard on the mouth, then dived from the window, rolling onto the ground and crouching low.

No time to protest. No time to process. Jody bounded from the window and stayed low next to Evan. The woods surrounded them, but they also masked whoever was trying to kill them. The sniper? Someone new? How had they been tracked? Jody's mind buzzed, but her lips tingled from that frantic, desperate kiss.

The wind howled through the trees and she shivered. Smoke clung to the air, masking any other scent. If someone was nearby, Jody couldn't smell him.

The moon gave off little light, but the flames engulfing the cabin shone a fiery spotlight on them. "We have to move fast. Let's go south. There's a ranger station. I'm not sure where exactly, but I know there is one. Along the river. We can find some shelter maybe and hide until first light."

Evan nodded and they scrambled into the woods as a gunshot fired. Bark splintered and rained down on Evan's head. "Stay low and run!"

Jody raced through the woods, tripping over fallen limbs, leaves crunching beneath her feet, but she was thankful for fresh air. She gulped it in as they ran south.

Another shot fired and hit a tree about five feet away. Either the shooter was a bad shot or the night blinded him, which meant he wasn't using night goggles. "Zigzag!" she whispered.

"Right behind you," Evan snapped back.

No point in reminding him that she was supposed to be covering him. She zigged right...

zagged left, her legs pushing harder. She hurdled a log and moved faster, Evan right on her heels.

About half a mile more and Jody slowed, then took cover behind a tree. "No more gunfire."

"You think we lost him?"

They'd eaten up about two miles of ground. Guess Evan hadn't given up cross-country running, either. She wasn't out of breath, but she was drained. The adrenaline had slowed and she was crashing. Sweat dripped from her brow and she wiped it with her shirt. "We have to get warm or we'll get a chill."

"Smoke and fire will draw the shooter to us."

They couldn't sit out there all night. The temperature was in the twenties. "Jackets in the backpacks." She'd been thorough.

Evan rummaged through his blue pack and retrieved an army jacket. Better than nothing. Jody grabbed an identical one, a little big but she'd snuggle into it. When their body temperatures dropped, they were going to freeze.

"Let's hoof it and see if we can't find a safe place to get through the rest of the night," Evan said. They trekked south, stopping periodically to listen, Jody to smell. Nothing out of the ordinary.

"Evan, how did someone find us? I thought maybe the computer, but I had a feeling we were being watched before anyone would have had time to track us through an IP address." Jody dug in the backpack and retrieved a bottle of water. She sipped and put it back inside.

"I know it wasn't the computer. I was cautious, I promise. The only thing I can think of is someone must have put a tracker on the SUV at CCM, especially if they saw you packing it up before they shot at us."

Jody tugged the jacket tighter around her. "Or they followed us from CCM." But she hadn't seen a tail. "Or put a tracker on the SUV at the gas station when we stopped for snacks and gas. That way they could fall back and we wouldn't have been alerted to their presence."

"The only way to know for sure is to double back to the cabin and check the Suburban."

"Unless they swiped it to remove any trace of evidence." Jody fisted a hand. "I hate not knowing anything definitive."

"Me, too." Evan placed a hand on her shoulder. "Look." He pointed to a thicket. "Let's set up here tonight. It's secluded and we've been walking awhile."

"We need fire."

"I know. I hate to chance it, though, but…" Evan shivered. "We have to or we'll freeze." He busied himself with creating a pit while Jody gathered wood. He retrieved a lighter from his backpack and lit the kindling. A small fire blazed and Jody held her hands out, thankful for the heat.

"If we double back tomorrow, don't you think they'd expect that from us?" She scooted closer to the fire, the light illuminating Evan's face—the day-old growth on his cheeks and chin reminded her of the scrape on her skin when he'd kissed her. Should she bring it up? Reprimand him?

"I'm not sure because I don't know who we're dealing with. Are they smart enough to guess our next move? Pros? Amateurs?" He tossed a twig in the fire. "Can you call Wilder? Have him meet us at the cabin."

Jody scowled. "I had two burner phones. One is on the coffee table burned to ash and the other is in the SUV console. For an emergency."

She should have packed one in each backpack but she had assumed they'd have one on them. Never dreamed they'd be smoked out of the cabin. That's what she got for assuming. "I'm sorry."

"Don't be. We'll trek to the SUV in the morning. Call Wilder and I'll relocate. Alone this time."

"You need someone to watch your back, Evan. You can't go rogue."

"I am sick of having this discussion. I'm risking your life. Your reputation." He flinched at his words.

"Then stop having it. I'm here. End of story.

My choice. And while we're on things to stop, you can't kiss me, Evan. What was that?"

"I don't know." He jumped up, paced. "I know what you said. And I agree—there is no future for us. But that doesn't mean I don't care about you. It doesn't mean I'm not afraid for you. I am all of those things. I got scared and reacted." He crumpled by the fire and hung his head between his knees. "I'm confused."

Join the club.

"You hate me and yet here you are fighting for me. I don't know what to do with that."

"I guess accept it." She couldn't explain it herself. After everything, the last person Jody should want to protect was Evan. But all she wanted was to make sure he lived. Was safe. Exonerated. She didn't know what to do with that, either. Love and hate was a blurry line. And she was riding right down the middle.

No, that wasn't true. "I don't hate you, Evan." Not anymore. Three years ago she had. Hate had left her bruised and battered, gaping from brutal wounds. But time had ebbed and those wounds had scabbed, leaving her now only tender to the touch and colored with reminders of the battle she'd gone through.

"But you won't forgive me," he murmured.

"I don't know if I can." Forgiving meant saying what he did was okay. Harboring the bitterness was eating her from the inside out. "Just promise you won't kiss me again."

He held her gaze, the blue of his eyes flickering in the firelight.

"I can't," he rasped. "Because the truth is I might. The truth is I want to kiss you every moment, every day. I want to kiss you right now. And I know I shouldn't. I know it can't lead anywhere. I know we're done for…but I still want to."

A lump formed in her throat. "Well, don't," she managed to say, her insides fevering.

Silence hung and Evan toyed with a stick. Finally he threw it in the fire. "Are you seeing anyone?"

"I'm not talking about my relationships with you, Evan." The fact that she hadn't dated anyone since him wasn't his business. Trust didn't come easy and she'd been afraid to put herself out there. Besides, she'd regretted the kind of relationship she and Evan had shared. She wouldn't let it happen again.

"I haven't seen anyone since you."

"Evan," she insisted. "You don't owe me your dating history. Can we please get off this subject?" She was nearly in tears.

He nodded. "Sure. I'll keep watch and the fire going."

Maybe this fire, but theirs had died, and nothing was left but cold ash.

EIGHT

Evan hadn't slept much. Each time the fired died and the cold settled in he'd woken and stoked it. Why couldn't he let the past go and accept that Jody wasn't going to forgive him? He couldn't escape the truth. Evan wasn't over Jody, not by a long shot. She was as strong as she'd ever been. She'd moved on with her life. Worked in a respectable job. Now she was going the distance and risking her life for him. She hadn't taken an oath like in the Secret Service. She did this by choice and it unraveled every cord inside him.

If he knew for certain he could be a better man, if he knew he could keep from hurting her, he might beg and plead for another shot. But she wouldn't even forgive him. She would never be able to look at him without thinking about what he'd done in the past, and she refused to discuss it. She was right, though. He shouldn't have kissed her.

He made sure the fire was completely out and

then he woke her. "Hey," he whispered. "Time to get going."

Jody massaged her neck and winced. "What time is it?"

"Seven fifteen. You up for the hike back to the SUV?"

She stood, stretched. "Give me a minute or two?"

He nodded and she grabbed her backpack and darted into the woods. A few minutes later she returned.

"We need to head back north." He unzipped his pack and pulled out a granola bar. "You hungry?" He knew she wouldn't be. She never ate first thing in the morning. Only coffee.

"I'd kill for a cup of coffee."

He grinned. "Me, too." He bit into his granola bar. "But try to eat soon. We need the energy."

They hiked in comfortable silence for about an hour. The sound of motorbikes roared in the distance. The trails out here were perfect for a day of dirt biking, but it was a bit cold for it this early in the day.

Jody paused. "You don't think…?"

"That whoever shot at us last night bought dirt bikes to find us?" Evan wouldn't bank on it, but then he was worth two million bucks. People had done crazier things for less money.

The roaring ripped through the air. Two red-

and-white dirt bikes with riders in dark helmets and black eye protectors crested the hill.

The one in front reached behind him.

"Duck!" Jody yelled, and shoved Evan behind a tree.

Shots fired.

"We only have so many bullets and who knows how many people are out here. Conserve. If we have to clip them, fine. But only if necessary." Evan pointed for Jody to dart through the woods; the dirt bikes followed.

"Get off the main trail, make it hard for them!" Evan yelled over the ripping and roaring of the motorcycles. Jody rushed off the trail and into the dense foliage, Evan following close behind.

Veering off the path didn't deter the motorbikes. They were built for this terrain.

Bullets exploded in their direction.

Evan circled back north, but they couldn't shake these guys.

Racing downhill, he and Jody jumped fallen limbs and tree stumps. The riders had split up now, hedging them in and herding them as if leading them farther away from the SUV.

Evan couldn't be sure if these riders were the same people who had burned down the cabin or if a new set of crazy assassins was after them. But the biggest question was—if there was more than one pair of killers, how had they all found

Evan and Jody? Evan itched for a laptop, a way to connect with the cyber world.

Another shot fired.

Pop!

Pop!

Jody's foot snagged on a fallen limb and she fell, rolling down the hill before Evan could catch her.

Evan sprinted toward her.

The sound of motorbikes grew closer.

Jody lay on her back, holding her knee, pain scrunching her face. Blood seeped through her khaki cargo pants.

"Can you walk?" The engines grew even louder. They would be spotted any moment. His heart kicked up a notch.

"I—I think so."

They had mere seconds before they were caught.

Jody couldn't run.

He scanned the forest and eyed an old dead tree that had fallen. "Come on!" He snatched her into his arms and raced to it. "It's going to stink in there for you, but you'll have to deal." Lowering her inside the hollowed-out trunk, he squeezed her hand. "I'll be right over there. Stay down."

Jody winced but nodded. The smell of dead wood and animals must be doing a number on her senses, but he had no other option. He bolted to a cluster of bushes and dived behind them, thistles stabbing through his clothing. He bit back a wince.

The dirt bikes came into view, slowing down. Searching. Evan crouched into a ball, trying to become invisible. *God, please don't let them see us. Hide us. Shelter us.*

It felt like time was stretching to a complete stop. The low hum of the bikes continued as they searched through the woods. Evan's breath had turned ragged. How bad was Jody's wound? If she couldn't walk it was a total game-changer.

The dirt bikes revved up and drove back through, slowing in front of him.

He crouched lower.

Didn't breathe.

Didn't move.

One of the bikes revved its engine and rode out of the woods, but one stayed behind. The motorbike idled, then slowly moved toward the hollowed-out tree.

Evan had drawn his weapon, prepared to lose a few bullets, when the motorbike sped up and by the tree.

Evan waited a beat.

Two.

Made sure they weren't circling back. When it was safe, he slipped from the brush to the dead tree he'd hidden Jody inside.

"I think they're gone."

Jody pushed herself up from the tree, gun in hand. Her pants were torn on the thigh. She separated the tear for a better look. "Great," she muttered. "I think I landed on a tree stump when I fell. It's not good, Evan."

He knelt and looked at her, asking for silent permission to examine the wound.

She nodded and he winced at the gash on her thigh. Blood and dirt hid the depth of the wound. He grabbed a bottle of water from his backpack and rinsed the cut. "You need stitches, Jo."

"I was afraid of that." She handed him her backpack. "My pack has a first-aid kit."

He rifled through and found it. "This is gonna hurt." He cleaned the wound and his hands, then took a sterile needle and thread. "You ready?"

She clamped her jaw. "Do it." Jody flinched and sucked in air through her teeth as the needle pierced her flesh.

"Sorry, Jo. You need about five."

She braced herself and he finished stitching her up, then applied an antibiotic ointment. With another needle and thread, he quickly sewed the pants back together to help protect the wound from further debris and possible infection.

"Can you walk?" he asked, and helped her stand.

"It burns and my ankle is turned, but not so bad I can't get moving. I don't think we should attempt to head back to the cabin. They'll expect that. And why not? It *was* our plan." She winced again. "Let's keep going south. Find that ranger's station. By now Wilder has called…several times. Which means he'll know something is up, and if I know him, he's already fanning out to find us."

Good. He searched the ground and found a large limb. He grabbed it and sloughed off some bark before handing it to Jody. "Here. Walking stick."

She accepted it and tried it out. "Thanks."

Evan stayed behind in case she lost her footing. That leg would be on fire from the stitches and tightness. Jody wasn't a complainer and was tough as nails. He'd always admired that about her. The hike sloped downhill. Plus for her.

About thirty minutes in, he stopped. "Let's take a breather."

She wouldn't admit she needed rest. Instead, she'd push herself further than necessary. They drank some water. The sun was bright but the wind was biting. The constant movement was the only thing keeping them from shivering. "I wish we knew how far the ranger's station was. It's like hiking blind. And we don't know if those guys will come back."

Jody sat on a tree stump and rubbed around her wound, then popped a couple ibuprofens.

"How would more than one person know where we are? It would make sense that whoever shot at us at CCM tracked the SUV or followed us—and did a good job because neither of us caught it. But the dirt bikes feel…like maybe someone else." With no way to reach the outside world, they'd stay clueless. "I guess we trust God to keep us safe."

Jody grunted and sipped on her water.

What happened with her friend in the Middle East had done a number on her. They'd discussed this often when they were together, but never through the lens of faith—which had clearly been affected, and he wondered how much *he* had affected that faith. Back then it wouldn't have crossed his mind. He never thought he'd done anything wrong. But now…he felt responsible. "Hey, Jo?"

"What?"

"Do you still believe? In God?"

Jody capped her water bottle and tucked it in her backpack. "I've always believed in God. I'm just not sure He cares as much as I thought He did when I was a kid." She shrugged.

Evan wasn't sure if he should speak up or not. He was fairly new to faith. "Is it…is it my fault?" The thought seared into his chest. His father had never wanted his mother to go church, and for years she hadn't. Evan would have never forbidden Jody's church attendance or public faith, but he'd never done anything to help her live it out, either. He wouldn't have had a clue how.

Jody adjusted her pack and stretched out her bad leg. "Evan, I was angry at God because no matter how hard I prayed or did the right thing, bad stuff still happened. Justice wasn't served. People, including myself, were hurt. When we met…you filled an empty place."

His head spun. He hadn't been in a new believer's class long to learn that God had to fill all the empty places. He'd used alcohol and partying. Jody… Jody had used him. And he'd let her. "Then it was me."

Jody's blues softened with sincerity and compassion. "No, Evan. It wasn't you. It was me. I can't blame anybody for the way I lived but myself."

"I made it easier, though, didn't I? Because I wasn't a believer then."

She stood, keeping her weight on the walking stick. "Not intentionally. Every mistake I ever made with you was my decision alone. Being with you was my choice. I knew you weren't a believer. I knew you played hard and fast. Don't blame yourself for that, okay?"

It was something. But still Evan felt guilty. "I'm sorry anyway. I'm not that guy anymore. Whether you believe it or not."

"I know you're not." She brushed a strand of hair from her eyes and the truth showed clearly. She did believe him. "Let's get moving. We don't know if those guys will come back for another round. For two million, I would." She grinned and the atmosphere instantly lightened.

Evan chuckled and quietly prayed that Jody would find her faith again, and this time he could be a help and not a hindrance.

Jody's leg throbbed and was on fire. She hoped it wasn't leading to infection. They'd walked for hours with a few stops in between. So far they'd been safe by staying off the main hiking trails. It was easier to avoid people altogether. Any face could be a killer's.

They'd eaten beef jerky and a couple packs of tuna for lunch but it was now long gone, and while she hated to admit she couldn't go any farther, she couldn't.

Too much weighed on her mind. Evan had felt bad about his part in her past. He reminded her of Locke when he was a little boy and felt bad about breaking one of her Barbies. Wide-eyed and hopeful things could be fixed.

She was glad that Evan was a man of faith. Here he was trusting God with countless, faceless killers after him, along with being framed, and instead of giving up on God, Evan was reciting Scripture and praying. And he didn't seem nearly as freaked-out as Jody. Evan was being stripped bare and leaning on God. Jody had been stripped bare, too, but instead she'd become insubordinate. Following commands and orders in the navy and in God's army had gotten her no-where. But taking matters into her own hands and making up her own rules hadn't panned out, either.

Everything inside ached. She'd asked God time and again why these things had to happen, but she got no answer. No answer had meant God didn't care. But…maybe she was wrong. Maybe no answer was an answer. A call to trust even in silence.

Evan grabbed her shoulder. "Hey, is that a cabin up there?"

Jody squinted against the sun and studied the woods. "I think so."

"You thinking what I'm thinking?" he asked.

"That depends. Are you thinking we squat for the night and start again in the morning?" she asked, hoping that was his thought.

Evan nodded and motioned her forward. "That's exactly what I'm thinking. It's set so far back, unless someone is familiar with the woods or an excellent tracker, we ought to be well hid-den."

For a while anyway.

"What if it's not abandoned?"

"We'll cross that bridge when we get there. Besides, you need off that leg and ankle." They hiked through the dense forest and toward the cabin. No sign of occupancy. "Stay here. I'll scope it out."

She didn't argue. If it was a dangerous situation, Jody couldn't sprint. She waited behind a pine tree while Evan stalked to the small hunting cabin. A few minutes later he returned. "It's empty. I kicked the back door in."

"We'll leave a sorry note." She snickered as Evan winked and led her around back. "Wow." Old smells of fish and animals had been left behind, along with something rancid and musty. "This is nasty. A man's cabin."

"Hey," Evan protested teasingly. "You're right. Total hunter's cabin."

The small cabin was comprised of an open kitchen, eating area and living room. One bathroom. One bedroom. "There are more deer heads and antlers than one person should ever see hanging on a wall in their lifetime. Not to mention mounted fish and dark green plaids." Jody shuddered.

"Well, it's better than hunkering down in the elements tonight. I don't think starting a fire is wise."

"I'm kinda over fire right now anyway." She groaned and laughed as she opened her backpack. One set of dry clothes in a waterproof bag. Unsure of how many days they had left of rugged living, she decided not to change. Instead, she excused herself to the bathroom to freshen up with the toothpaste and deodorant she'd packed them. Some days her obsessive sense of organizing paid off.

They had a few packs of dehydrated meals, snacks and a couple cans of soup and beanie weenies. At some point they needed to get to that ranger's station or to a road where they could hitch a ride into the nearest town and get a hotel room or a pick up from Wilder. He was probably going out of his mind.

"Jo?"

"Yeah," she hollered from the small bathroom.

"I found a rifle. Guess what I'm thinking?"

"That we should shoot everyone in our path and haul it to civilization and safety? And then order a pizza?" She was starving for Italian sausage and layers of mozzarella.

Evan laughed from the other side of the door. "I was thinking rabbit or squirrel. I found a generator, too. We have power."

"Good deal on the power, but it's illegal to shoot animals—even for food—in a state park."

"Not all parks."

Yeah, well, they had no way of knowing if this was one of them. "But some."

"Beanie weenies in a can it is. But when we leave, I'm taking this gun and the two hunting knives in the drawer."

"We'll add it to our sorry list." Jody checked the wound Evan had stitched. Her thigh was swollen and red but it didn't appear fevered or infected. Yet. She opened the door. Evan stood close. Looking every bit the rugged mountain man—the kind in commercials, not in back-woods movies.

"What?" he asked.

Busted admiring him. "You smell."

His sly grin tipped her heart on its side. "It's called masculinity."

It took her a moment to find her voice. "It's called sweat and two days of not showering." Granted, he did have an earthy smell running along his skin, but he wasn't ripe. But she needed some distance. "So steer clear of me."

"Mmm-hmm…no promises."

He blocked her path, his hands resting on the lintel of the door as he held her gaze. He didn't believe a word she was saying. "Don't get cocky. It doesn't suit you." But it so did.

"Again…" His voice turned husky. "No prom-ises."

Why did that look, that smirk, that voice send her for a loop even after all this time? Duck-ing under his arm, she slipped into the living area. He entered the bathroom and shut the door. When he came out he smelled like fresh deodor-ant, the cleaning wipes from their backpacks and pretty much irresistible. Jody found her vapor rub and swiped it under her nose. He wasn't fighting fair.

Or maybe Jody was warring with herself. Fighting the attraction and feelings.

"Do you think the authorities have figured out Wilder owns a cabin and have checked it?" Jody asked.

"I haven't heard helicopters. If they found it burned down they'd suspect foul play. They'd bring choppers or drones. We'll have to keep our eyes peeled." He opened up a couple of cans of beans and hot dogs, then dug around in the cabinets for a bowl. After wiping it out, he dumped in the contents and slid it into an ancient microwave.

It beeped and Evan brought the bowl and two forks to the table. "Bon appétit."

Jody snorted and they shared the bowl. Like they had many times—only it wasn't beanie weenies. "Once we find the ranger's station and get Wilder's help, have you thought about that boat idea?"

Evan toyed with his fork. "I don't know, Jo. I'm going to ask Wilder to get me a new laptop, and maybe I'll hole up in Mexico. Work until I can figure out who Lawman1 is and how I can take him down and prove my innocence. If I could get his hard drive, get his private emails, then I'd have him. But he could be anyone. He could live anywhere in the world. And I still can't make myself believe that anyone in my field office—on my task force—is behind this. Clive Bevin doesn't have the technical ability—"

"If you only have to download the browser and the software that keeps you anonymous and untraceable, then all he'd need is to private message Lawman1. What other technical ability would he need?"

Evan's mouth formed a hard, grim line, and he put his fork down and pushed the bowl toward Jody. "None. But Clive? Terry? Any of them? I wish we could call Wheezer and see what he's found on them financially. No one is rich in this profession but some are further in debt than others, and the offer of money in exchange for information could be tempting."

"Anyone have a new car? New purchases that would stand out?" Jody asked, and picked through the beans for the hot dogs.

"No." But anyone with half a brain would know to keep that on the down low. "We should probably turn in early so we can start before first light."

Jody agreed, but there was no way she was going to get a good night's rest. Not when there was a killer or killers on the hunt for Evan. Not when her brain and heart were playing a terrible game of chicken. They were going to collide, and Jody was going to be wrecked.

Again.

NINE

Evan slowed his pace. Jody was trying to cover her limp, but the leg injury from yesterday wasn't cooperating. His stitch job wasn't fantastic, either, but once they made it to civilization they could have it checked.

It was after two o'clock. He and Jody had slept in. The secluded cabin had given them a measure of security and they'd needed the rest. Evan had taken the threadbare couch and Jody had slept on the twin bed in the only bedroom.

An hour ago, they'd stumbled upon the Chattahoochee River and Evan couldn't help it; he'd hummed the old country song, trying to lighten the mood. While the sun was bright and full, the wind was strong, especially near the river. Their hiking had kept their body temperatures up but it was cold. In the thirties, if he had to guess. With the shade from the forest it felt like it was in the twenties.

Following the current, Evan hoped they'd

reach a ranger's station by nightfall. They didn't have proper shelter for another night in the elements and they hadn't seen a cabin since they'd left the one earlier today. Jody hadn't spoken much. Probably concentrating on her footsteps. And if he knew her well, which he did, she was formulating ideas on how to convince him to hitch a boat to the water and brave the sea for a while—and how to convince him to let her join him.

His stomach rumbled. They hadn't eaten much—trying to conserve. "Jo, how's the leg?"

"Working," she said in a clipped tone. Was she angry or concentrating? Probably irritable from uncomfortable sleep arrangements and her leg.

"You think we can—"

The sound of something whizzing right above his shoulder stopped his statement. Two feet in front of him he spotted what it was.

An arrow.

Jody gawked at the arrow, then at Evan and to the trees behind him. "Is that—"

Fwoop!

Another arrow.

Evan yanked Jody up the bank into the cover of trees.

"Are—are we being hunted like animals?" Jody whispered.

"Appears so." Evan scanned the area. Couldn't make out where the hunter might be. The arrows looked expensive. Well made. "We have to haul it. Can you run?"

"Do I have a choice?" She frowned and darted a glance behind Evan. "Go first. I'm right behind you."

This again. "I don't think so. You're wounded. You need cover and this guy is probably already moving in on us as we speak. Now. Go." *God, be with us.* "Right through that thicket of trees. We can use them as shields."

Another arrowed pierced the tree an inch above Jody's head. Missed shot? Or was the marksman aiming for her? If so, why?

Jody yanked it from the tree and dashed ahead, clutching the arrow and moving pretty fast for someone with an injured leg. Evan tore off after her.

Tree limbs with bare, sharp twigs caught his shirt, ripping it and stabbing into his flesh, but he pressed on. The only sounds were their breathing and the crunching of brush under their feet.

Another arrow flew, barely missing Jody.

He might be a hunter. The woods would be his friend. Evan's pulse thumped in his temples. They couldn't stay in the forest and lose the killer.

Ten feet out the trees opened up to the riverbank. The waters churned violently, the current strong. Jagged rocks jutted to the surface, dark and slick.

How many killers were out in these woods?

Evan's insides constricted and nausea nipped at the back of this throat, his gut churning like the waters before him.

Jody's eyes were wide. Her body shaking. "We have no choice, Evan."

Evan eyed the river. "No way. It's freezing. The current's powerful. We might not survive." The distance to the other side might as well be three hundred feet in this weather.

"We'll most certainly die if we go back into the woods. He'll track us. Like animals."

An arrow soared through the air, barely missing Jody. Jody again? "Okay." Every nerve in Evan's body burned and jackhammered inside him. He clicked his backpack straps across his chest so he wouldn't lose it in the river.

Jody was running for the banks and plunging into the icy waters. Evan followed as an arrow hit his backpack.

Oh, God, help us! Evan jumped in, the freezing river water shocking his system, sucking away his breath. The current pulled him under and he fought to the surface for oxygen, searching for Jody, but the river took him hostage again, ravaging him and hurtling him downstream at a fast and furious pace.

"Ev!"

Jody's voice!

He slammed into a rock, jarring his ribs. Fire

blazed through his bones as spots danced before his eyes, but he used all he had to fight going under and downriver.

They had to get across.

Now.

Up ahead, Jody clung to a boulder jutting from the river. "Give me your hand!" she called. Water sloshed over her head, matting her hair to her face, but she held on with one arm, the other outstretched.

Evan kicked his legs and prayed. If he could just get to her...

He neared her.

He had one opportunity to grab on.

What if he pulled her off and they both went to a watery grave?

Could he risk it?

"Don't you even think it!" she hollered. The woman had an uncanny ability to read his thoughts. "Grab my hand!"

Evan channeled all his strength and propelled himself toward her.

Now or never.

He stretched out his hand and she gripped it like iron, but the current was strong and tried to separate them.

"Don't you let go, Evan Anthony Novak!"

Jody's hand was slipping off the rock.

"I can't risk—" water raced over his head "—you drowning."

"Then get up here!" she screamed as if he was still a recruit in boot camp.

He swung his free hand up and over, clutching a jagged piece of the boulder, and hoisted himself next to Jody. "Thank you," he said, his voice weak and hoarse, his teeth chattering. Jody's lips were blue and quivering.

A long tree branch hung over the raging water about five feet away on the other side. If they could find a way to get to it, they could shimmy onto the branch and jump to shore. The current had ushered them downriver at a wild pace. They had time to try to figure it out. But it wouldn't be long before the bow hunter made it to them.

"Get...get...in-inside my pack," Jody said through shivers and chattering teeth. "I have...a rope. Gonna swing it onto...onto...the branch... over...there."

A rope. *Score!*

He could kiss her. He hadn't made any promises he wouldn't.

Jody shifted in the water to give Evan access to her backpack. He clung with one hand and opened the backpack with the other. Water rushed inside it, robbing them of food packs. Using his arm, he lifted himself and the backpack farther out of the water. He found the rope and shoved it between his teeth while he used his free hand to zip the pack back up.

Climbing to the top of the rock, his foot slipped.

He was returned to the freezing river, but he caught the rock's edge and Jody clung to his hand.

Once again he tried to climb, the water racing over his boots keeping him off balance.

He had to get that rope over the branch with enough force it would swing around and around the limb, securing it for their weight.

Grunting, he swung it like a lasso to gain momentum.

God, let it be enough.

Like David with a sling and a few rocks, Evan aimed and launched the rope over the branch; it looped over once…twice…a third time.

Yes! Thank You, God!

He glanced down. "Jo, you making it, hon?"

Her nod was weak.

"Up you go, then." He held out his hand for her. With an injured thigh and ankle, her footing would be wobbly at best. "Clasp the rope and swing over to the bank, then toss it back to me."

Jody grabbed the rope and peered into his eyes, lips quivering. "My legs…feel…like lead."

"I know. But you can do this and I'll meet you on the other side." And then they could figure out what in the world to do to raise their body temperatures. "You want a push?"

She shook her head. Of course not. This was the bravest woman he'd ever met. She'd muster the strength. Draw it out from deep within. "Jo, I know you're not happy with God right now, but you should pray."

She met his eyes—could be water, could be tears—but she actually nodded and muttered a prayer for help across, and then she sprung off the rock and swung like Jane in a Tarzan movie. Her landing wasn't as powerful, but she'd reached the shore.

And she'd prayed to God. That alone gave him the strength he needed.

She reared back and thrust the rope back across; Evan barely grabbed it, wound it around his hands and pushed off the rock.

Halfway across, the rope slipped loose.

He plunged into the water.

Two feet shy of the rock that could help him the rest of the way.

Jody watched in horror as the driving current hurled Evan away. She jumped to her leaden feet and raced down the bank—the fire in her thigh searing into her bones while the wintry chill left goose bumps in its wake.

"Evan! Hold on! I got you!" Vain words. He was rushing downriver and she was barely keeping up with him. There had to be a way to reach him. To save him!

God.

God could help her. If He could part the Red

Sea and the Jordan River, He could surely save Evan from the Chattahoochee!

Did she trust Him to?

When thou passest through the waters, I will be with thee; and through the rivers, they shall not overflow thee.

The verse struck her so powerfully it might as well have been God's audible voice.

He was here.

Near.

Hadn't left her.

Hadn't forsaken her.

Tears sprang to her eyes as she barreled down the banks. The hard crust over her heart melted like it had been exposed to a summer day. Up ahead, Evan bobbed in the water. Under. Surfaced. Under again… Repeat… He was fighting.

The feeling of God right beside her moved her faster, farther.

God is our refuge and strength, a very present help in trouble.

The psalm sprang inside like a fever. "Oh, God, we need You. *I* need You. Evan needs You." She wasn't quite the protector she believed herself to be. She didn't have the power to always rescue. But He did.

Evan spiraled so far down the river she feared she'd lose sight of him.

Lose *him*.

The reality that he could die and she'd never

see him again, never be able to voice what he wanted to hear—that she forgave him—fueled another dose of adrenaline as she dashed down the bank, scanning the area for something to help him.

The minute she'd called on God, the bitterness dissolved. Like Moses throwing the branch into bitter water and making it sweet. She had been like that branch. Soaked in God's grace and forgiveness, and now she had the strength to admit she forgave Evan.

But she needed to be able to tell him.

Up ahead lay a long dead limb. If she could thrust it in the water, he might be able to grab on and she could pull him safely to shore. "Evan, try to get closer to me." She drove harder. Her leg didn't protest, as if God Himself was giving her the power and strength to race against time.

She grabbed the heavy limb. *God, give me strength*. She thrust it into the river and Evan's arms moved, pumping himself toward her. He wouldn't be able to take the freezing waters for long before everything shut down.

Jody held the branch, her heart racing. *Come on. Come on*.

The waters jerked him under.

Held him.

No.

"Evan!" *Fight. Come on. Fight*.

Thirty seconds passed.

A minute.

Blood whooshed in Jody's ears. She frantically scanned the waters, searching for any sign of Evan.

"Evan! Evan!" she hollered, not caring that they were being hunted. Stalked. She squeezed her eyes shut, tears leaking out, a strangled sob erupting from her throat.

God, I trust You!

A heavy weight tugged on the branch.

Her eyes popped open.

Evan's head surfaced and the sound of his lungs greedily taking in air rose over the water. Over the blood in her ears.

Thank You, God. Thank You!

Jody yanked on the limb, drawing Evan in until he reached the shore and crumpled beside her, weak. Drenched. Heaving breaths.

She wrapped her arms around him. He was alive. Alive and right here safe on the shore.

Sobs forced their way from her mouth and she clung to him. "I forgive you. I forgive you, Evan. But if you ever scare me like that again, I'll hold it against you forever."

He hacked and coughed, raised his head to peer into her eyes. "You forgive me?" he asked breathlessly.

"I forgive you."

He brushed the hair from her eyes. "Thank you. Who knew all I had to do was have a near-death experience." A lopsided grin turned her heart upside down.

He continued to lock his eyes on hers.

"Jo," he whispered.

If he asked permission to kiss her she'd cave and lie here on the shores freezing to death. But her lips would be warm and her insides ablaze. She couldn't kiss him. Forgiveness did not equal trust. And while she knew without a shadow of a doubt he'd protect her from danger, she still didn't trust him with her heart. She couldn't.

"Yeah?"

"We have to get somewhere warm. Get dry."

Right. He wasn't even thinking about kisses. He'd wanted her forgiveness and she'd given it. But he'd agreed with her earlier that they didn't have a future together. He stood, then helped her to her feet. "We don't know how much time we have."

Between hunters and the elements, and them soaking wet—not much.

"We have dry clothes in the waterproof bags," Jody said.

A crack split the atmosphere.

Jody felt the force hit her. "I've been hit!"

Evan grabbed her, hauled her into the forest.

"No…my backpack's been hit," she said as they ran for cover. "It must have struck the canned goods."

Several bullets fired.

"Stay low!" Evan hollered and trailed close behind, shielding her. "They don't care who they hit."

Jody had noticed that earlier. Before, Evan was clearly the target. Now it seemed it didn't matter. The thought slammed into her as hard as that bullet had made impact with her backpack. Could Jody have been added to the hit list?

Jody moved so fast her feet almost came out from under her.

Safety. Safety. *God, lead us to safety.*

The smells of earth and iron smacked her senses. Iron…her leg must be bleeding again. She must have pulled the stitches loose or something. Still, she pushed forward, weaving through the woods. No rhyme or reason to it. No destination.

Up ahead lay a rocky crag covered in dense gnarly kudzu branches and moss. "Do you see that?" Jody pointed to the hole in the center of the crag. Big enough for a man to fit inside. "Looks like the mouth of a cave." There were many caves in Georgia, but this small opening seemed abandoned, which meant it was off-limits to the public due to hazards inside.

No choice for them.

"Get down in there. Go!" Evan shoved her into the small opening. She wiggled through into the darkness. Decomp. Stagnant water. Earth. Must. She pulled the vapor rub from her zipped pocket and smeared a little under her nose. She couldn't even see her hand in front of her face.

Something touched her shoulder and she jumped.

"It's me. Sit tight. I'm going to pull those limbs across the opening. Just in case." She needed to reach out, touch something solid, but fear held her back. Bugs. Bats. Any creepy crawler living in the darkness kept her hands to her sides.

Evan grunted as scraping sounded at the lip of the cave. "Got it," he whispered, and a few seconds later she smelled his scent and felt his touch to her shoulder. "I have a lighter in the waterproof bag but I'm afraid to move or make noise right now."

If they were heard, they were dead.

If the opening was spotted and the killers were smart enough to know they'd taken their chances on a cave that might house dangerous animals— they were dead.

If one of those animals sniffed them out...

All Jody could think about was the fact that any minute they might be dead.

TEN

Evan shivered next to Jody until it was clear they were safe for the time being. His fingers could barely work due to the cold. His eyes wouldn't adjust. Too dark. He fumbled in his backpack and found the lighter. Pulling it from the waterproof bag, he sparked it and everything illuminated before him. Which was what he'd expected to happen in his heart when Jody had breathed words of forgiveness on the shore earlier.

For a moment he was ecstatic, but as the minutes ticked by while he stood quietly waiting for the killers to move on, those same old whispers hissed into his ears. He was exactly like Dad. A Judas. A man who hurt the woman he claimed to love—which Evan had already done to Jody, proving those whispers to be true. Giving his life to God may have saved him eternally, but it hadn't changed his DNA.

"We have to get dry and warm, Evan. I'm

freezing and hypothermia is going to set in. My joints already feel paralyzed."

Evan agreed and held up a few broken branches he'd grabbed when covering the opening. "We may have to start a fire." Risky, but necessary. He cast the lighter and surveyed the cave. About eight feet high at the mouth, but it tapered off farther in. Five feet across. The space was tight. He forced his feet to work and moved deeper inside, Jody on his heels clinging to the little light. Limestone walls covered with guano. A few bats hung asleep. Bugs skittered across the cold, stone floor and up walls. "Okay, here's how this is gonna work. You go back behind that rock. I'm going to move to the lip of the cave, and we're going to change into dry clothes. Then we're going to move farther back. Hopefully it'll open up into a larger cavern and we can start a fire. We have to get warm. Take our chances."

Jody nodded and the lights went out. When Jody gave the okay, Evan returned with the flicker of the lighter and brought some sight to the place. "Watch your step. Hang on to my shirt if you need to. How's your leg?"

She gripped a fistful of his shirt. "I'm so cold I don't know if I'm in pain or not. Guess I'll know when I thaw."

Evan continued on. "Watch your head." Stalactites hung like piercing spears from the ceiling of the cave. The walls closed in and he grimaced.

Tight spaces didn't ring his bell. If it didn't widen soon, they'd have to turn back or come up with a new plan for warmth.

About twenty feet ahead, his shoulders relaxed. Space. Precious space.

The cave opened into an alcove about ten feet across, and two tunnels flanked either side of the cave. Now to start a fire. It wasn't exactly safe. There could be acidic gases in the air. "Jo, what do you smell?"

"Animal droppings, stagnant water, death…"

"Sulfur? And if so, how strong is it to someone like me?"

"A normal smeller?" She half laughed as she wrapped her arms around her middle and rubbed her upper arms, then inhaled. "I can smell it, but it's not repulsive or super heavy. I think we're safe lighting a fire."

"You don't think it'll ignite?"

"I don't think so, but I'm no speleologist." She surveyed their surroundings. "Okay. Here's to not blowing ourselves up."

Evan chuckled, but it wasn't too off base or funny. He breathed a prayer, lit the wood and flames came to life, shadows dancing off the ceiling and walls. Eerie.

Jody knelt by the fire and thrust her hands over it. "I can't tell you how good this feels."

"Belicve me, I know." Evan mimicked her and they warmed their bones in silence. The feeling came back to his fingers and toes in a burning sensation. The fire wouldn't last forever, though. He might have to go back out for more wood or burn something in their packs, which would cause a lot of smoke, but they had to stay warm.

"Thank you," he said after a while.

"For what?" she whispered. "Forgiving you or saving your life?"

Evan grinned. "Both." If only the words had brought the balm he desperately needed to his soul. "Because I really am sorry for what I did, though I know excuses are lame and don't change anything."

Jody hugged her knees. "No," she murmured. "Forgiveness doesn't renew trust, Evan. That takes time. A lot of time."

"I know." He cared about Jody more than anyone, and the best way to keep her heart intact was to steer clear of trying to secure it again. When he was twelve, his father had been dry for about six months. Mom had laughed a lot during that time and light had been in her eyes. But one night Dad came home and it was clear he'd been drinking. Evan had covered his head with a pillow and tried to tune out the arguing. The next day Dad had blamed his relapse on everything under the sun and apologized. But Evan knew he'd do it again. He would hurt Mom again. Hurt Evan. He stopped listening to excuses and apologies after that night.

He was sorry for what he'd done to Jody, but he wouldn't give himself the chance to hurt her again. "You feeling okay?"

"Yeah. Exhaustion is hitting me, though."

"I wish we knew what was happening."

"Me, too," she said.

"Hey, Jo?"

"Yeah."

"Why didn't you read the letter? And…will you now?" He'd poured everything into it. Wrote it dozens of times until he had the right words. Knew each one now by heart.

Jody sighed. "I can't."

"Why? If you've forgiven me."

"I ripped it up and threw it away."

"Oh… I guess I can't blame you."

"I'm sorry. I wish I had read it." She sniffed. "How's your mom?"

A personal question. Those had been few and far between these past days. Mom had always liked Jody. Told Evan to hang on to her.

"Good. She's seeing someone. A nice guy. I hope it works out and she's not alone anymore. I want her to be happy."

"That's nice to hear."

"Your mom? Doing well?" The small talk was strange.

"Mmm-hmm. I see her every other weekend. She's doing better each day without Daddy, but we miss him. Locke doesn't get out to visit much. But that's Locke." She rolled her eyes.

Evan had always liked Jody's younger brother, but he was an adrenaline junkie. "Is he ever gonna settle down?"

Jody laughed, and the rich alto tone echoed through the alcove. "Doubtful. He's in Alaska right now. Hoping to capture an avalanche on film. Mama stays in a state of panic over him. She wants him to get married, have 2.5 kids and become a wedding photographer—something safe." She laughed again. "He'll never do any of those things."

Evan would like to be a husband and father. If he could come out from under his family curse.

"But he can take a gorgeous photo of nature." Jody shrugged.

"Too bad he doesn't stick to meadows or prairies."

"He'd be happy to if it came with an F5 tornado in it," Jody quipped, then sat up straight. "I hear something," she whispered.

Evan heard it, too. Footsteps. Murmurs. His heart lurched into his throat and he jumped up. He pointed to a small crevice above. "Up. Go. We'll throw them off. Make them think we took one of those tunnels."

Jody's eyes widened. "What if something's up there?"

"Well, something is definitely down here and headed our way."

"Good point."

"I'll make it look like we've gone through that opening." Evan scrambled and dropped a wrapper inside the opening, then traced his footprints back to the site. Jody was already hoisting herself into the crevice on the rocky ledge.

Evan stomped out the final embers of the fire and used his lighter to make his way to the slippery limestone ledge, where he boosted himself up. "I don't think there's room in this space for the both of us," he whispered.

"Lay on your belly and back into it. That's what I did. Then roll on your side. If we face each other, we'll fit. But, Evan…it's a seriously tight space. Take a deep breath, okay?"

Blood whooshed in Evan's temples, but he pocketed the lighter and slowly backed into the ledge, the space narrowing until he felt the cold, slippery wall cut into his left shoulder and Jody's body rest against his right.

"Flip, Evan, or you'll wedge us in!" Jody hissed.

He shimmied and wiggled, but the space was tight already. Finally he managed to roll onto his left side, Jody's nose pressed against his, her breath blowing across his skin.

The alcove had excellent acoustics and whispers reached their ears.

A flashlight fanned across the cavernous walls and they pressed farther down. His lips grazed hers, but now was not the time to think romantically.

"Which way do you think they went?" a man whispered.

"I don't know. Should we split up? Gives us a better shot in case they have. Taking down one is better than none. I want the money." Another voice hissed.

Taking down one is better than none? The hit was on Evan.

Jody's breath faltered.

She was onto Evan's train of thought.

Jody had become a target. Had Lawman1 upgraded, offered more money and included her? Why?

"I want them both dead. I didn't off those two morons on dirt bikes to let one of these targets go."

They had killed the two men on motorbikes.

"Well, they definitely have been here. Started a fire. It's still warm, so they ain't been gone too long. Guess the update is correct. They're in this park. Somewhere."

Evan pressed his forehead into hers, as much to comfort her as to seek comfort. Their suspicions about their whereabouts being posted online was correct. These killers confirmed it.

"We can take 'em," Jody whispered, her mouth

moving against his and sending tingles down his spine. His arm was wedged across her waist. He could feel her chest rise and fall as she breathed.

"No." They would see it coming with their flashlights. There was a time to fight and a time to play it safe. Now was time to be safe. Listen. Hope for more information and that they'd follow the trails without finding them up in this crevice.

"You think they'd split up?" one of the men asked.

"I don't know. Site said they're both former soldiers and agents in law enforcement, so it won't be like she's scared to be alone. But we don't know how far in these tunnels go."

"Hey! Look. Footprints and brush. They went this way."

Footsteps and silence.

"Or they made it look like they did and they went inside that one. They'll be smart. Try to throw us off. By now they know they're as good as dead. Motorbikes and guns give it away. Morons, I say again. Let's go the opposite tunnel."

Footsteps sounded. When nothing could be heard, Evan touched her arm. "Let's get out of here." He wiggled and scooted until he was free from the crevice. His pulse immediately regulated. Jody squirmed her way out and dropped onto her good leg.

They hurried through the cave and came to the opening. Evan peered out.

Coast seemed clear.

But with their location and a huge sum of money on a hit site, it wouldn't stay clear for long.

Jody followed Evan, using trees as coverage, her chest pounding. Now she was a full-blown target. She'd shielded Evan at the convention center, been the source to identify a shooter at the hotel and she'd gotten him safely out of CCM. Looked like Lawman1 had had enough and thrown in Jody as a mark. It would make it easier to take down Evan if she were out of the picture.

They'd been trekking through the woods for about thirty minutes. Unable to stay along the river and out in the open, they still headed south toward the ranger's station. Every second in this park was a second closer to death. But it was good to be out of the cave, out of the crevice where she'd been entirely too close to Evan. Nose to nose. Mouth to mouth.

"Evan, can we slow down? My thigh is on fire."

Evan slackened his pace, then stopped and pulled a bottle of water from his pack. She was out, so he passed her the bottle for a sip. "Wilder is probably going out of his gourd, but he'll have some measure of comfort in the fact that our corpses aren't on the site and the Bitcoin is still sitting in that online wallet."

"True." Evan placed the water bottle back inside the pack. "I'm sure Wheezer has been monitoring that site 24/7. I wonder if he's gotten any closer to hacking into it and dissolving the account, or if he's made any headway with the offshore account Lawman1 made to look like mine."

Jody rubbed around the tender area on her leg. "I don't know, but we might be stupid for going to the ranger's station. If they've seen the news and your picture, they'll call the authorities the second they recognize you. Have you thought about that?"

"You may have to go alone and give them a cover story to use the phone and send Wilder in to help us. Since we haven't heard or seen any helicopters or drones, law enforcement hasn't discovered the cabin." Evan motioned for them to get moving again.

"Yet. They haven't figured it out yet." Jody smelled roasting meat and the hint of coffee brewing, then she detected smoke billowing from a campfire up ahead.

Evan blocked her. "Could be a killer."

"True, but it could be a camper."

She got the pointed look. "In January?"

"Maybe, if it's legal to bow hunt in the park. It's deer season." For once Jody hoped it would be someone safe. Her nerves were shot, she was afraid and flat-out exhausted, but there was no going back now. She was a target, too. "Do you have a gun? Mine got lost in the river."

"I put my Sig in the waterproof pack inside. It's safe. But I don't have a lot of bullets and the big weapons I lifted from the cabin were lost in the river."

What she wouldn't give for Wilder's arsenal right now. The wood smoke was intense. Her senses were on high alert and threatening a migraine—the last thing she needed right now. *God, since we're talking again, I'm asking for help.*

"We may not need bullets. We have the advantage. Let's get closer and scope it out."

They used the trees as camouflage as they crept up on the small navy pup tent. Leaning against it was a crossbow with a quiver of arrows—the same kind used to attack them.

Jody's hope deflated. Probably not a coincidence. On a line running from one tree to another were a couple of dead squirrels. Guess the guy was in survivalist mode with no intention of packing it in until he found Evan and Jody. Wonder if he knew two others were also out here and not only working to kill their targets but the competition, as well.

The guy had a camouflage hunting cap on, and wiry gray hair poked out. His belly was round and his face weathered. He looked like someone's grandpa, not a predator. "Let's go guns blazing," Jody whispered.

"Gun blazing. We have a gun not guns." Evan winked. Nice to see he still had some humor. Jody lost hers in the river with her Sig Sauer. And this might only take one bullet. Evan was a crack shot. "Let's scare him half to death, get some information, and then we'll figure out what to do with him. We can't let him go if he's a killer, and we can't drag him with us, either."

Jody was for the good guys winning and taking down bad guys, but she preferred to take them in alive. "Okay, you take the lead as I have no gun."

Evan nodded. "Let's go give grandpa a surprise."

"Surprise, Evan. Not heart attack. He might really be camping."

Cocking his head, he squinted. "You don't believe that do you?"

"I want to."

"Me, too. But the upside is we're down two hit men. We might only be up against the two men from the cave. We got this."

Twigs a few feet away snapped. Maybe the old man wasn't alone.

Gramps, the possible assassin, still sat in front of the fire warming himself.

Jody held her breath. Blood pounded in her

ears as Evan kept her shielded next to him as they crouched low, listening...waiting.

Whatever or whoever snapped the twigs came closer...

Closer...

They might have to use those bullets.

Evan's breathing was slow and even.

Waiting.

The noise came from behind a tree about five feet away.

Evan pointed, aimed.

A gray fluffy rabbit hopped through the leaves and Evan breathed a laugh. "I don't think Bugs has access to the hit site, do you?"

"Who knows at this point? Death by a rabbit. Anything is possible."

"Killer might have sicced a rabies-infested fluff ball on us." Evan buried his face in his forearm to suppress a laugh. They were delirious, plotting their own ridiculous demise. But a possible killer sat about ten feet away, and they needed information and hopefully a phone.

"Let's go have a chat with Mr. Crossbow."

"It's a nice crossbow, Jo. When we leave this site, I'm taking it with us." Evan grinned and it shocked her how much she could respond to him with everything else going on.

Evan aimed the gun on his target and he and Jody charged ahead, startling the old man, who scrambled for his crossbow. "This bullet is a lot faster than you, sir. I suggest you press Pause and put your hands up."

The old man slowly raised his hands, eyes wide. Maybe he was a camper. "We know what you're in these woods doing. I have a tear in my backpack to prove it," Evan said. "If you want to live, I suggest you tell us everything you know." Evan glanced down at the fire. "And pour us a cup of that coffee you're brewing."

Jody bit the inside of her cheek. Evan's cool demeanor and nonchalance with a criminal always surprised her. Of course, this man wouldn't scare a mouse. So why was he out here trying to kill them?

"P-p-please… I'm just hunting squirrels."

"With a crossbow?" Evan asked, and cocked his head.

The man eyed Jody before swinging his gaze back to Evan. His cheeks grew ruddier, and tears sprang in his eyes. Evan glanced at Jody. "I didn't even say anything that threatening."

She shook her head. "Sir, explain yourself. Why are you out here trying to kill us, and how did you know where to find us?" A whiff of Old Spice hit her. What poor man remembered to splash a little aftershave before a kill? This man was clearly not a trained assassin.

"I had to do it. I nced the money."

How would a guy his age even know about

the dark web and how to maneuver through it? "How did you hear about the hit?"

"Look," he said as tears continued to leak, "I needed some special help. My wife has cancer. I heard about these online places where you can buy…you know…drugs." He whispered the last words. Yes, saying *drugs* might be taboo, but taking out two human beings with a bow and arrow was okay. "I wanted to ease her pain. But then I discovered there's a lot of things on these sites. You wouldn't believe it."

"I assure you we would," Evan said drily. "And that's how you found a site that would pay you two million dollars to take me out."

He pointed to Jody. "Plus a million for her."

Jody's knees turned to water. "Go on," she said to the man.

"It said you'd last been spotted in this park. Gave a general location, but there was nothing but ashes there."

Must be the cabin. "So you decided to track us. You do realize we're not squirrels and you're going to prison for attempted murder."

The man crumpled, face to the ground. "My wife is dying! We're drowning in medical debt—"

"We were drowning in that icy river!" she hollered.

"I'm desperate," the man pleaded as his nose

ran and his eyes swelled from tears. "I can't go to prison. Who will take care of my wife? It's just us."

"I guess you should have thought about that before you decided to become a murderer." What were they gonna do with this guy?

"Do you have a cell phone?" Evan asked.

The man nodded. He was a broken mess, but Jody was having a tough time feeling sorry for him after he'd sent an arsenal of arrows their way, forcing them into the river to die. But still... crises could turn you into someone you weren't. Or bring out who you really were.

Jody snatched the man's phone. Only a couple of bars, but it'd do. She dialed Wilder's number. He answered on the first ring.

"Wilder Flynn."

"It's me."

"I was hoping so. Whose phone are you on? Never mind, Wheezer's tracing it now. You safe?"

"Yes. We're south of the cabin. It's been burned to the ground."

"I know. When you wouldn't answer the phone, we rode out there. Beckett is tracking you on foot now. But I've got a map on me. There's a clearing where I can land a chopper. I'm coming to get you."

Relief washed over Jody. "Beckett's tracking us," she said to Evan while Wilder gave her coordinates. She rattled them off to Evan. All they had to do was use the compass and head southeast. The river would take them to the rendezvous point. "I don't know how far we are from there. Or who we might encounter next." She told them how many miles south they'd trekked since the cave.

"According to the map, you're about ten miles from the cave. And twelve from the clearing. Without any interference, how fast can you hike? You injured?" Wilder asked.

"We can get there in two-and-a-half hours. And we're in working order."

"I texted Beckett. He found your cave dwelling already and has followed your trail. But you've got a few miles on him. I'll keep him tracking and watching your back. He found two dead men off a trail near the cave. Shot execution style."

Jody gave him the short version of their last forty-eight hours.

"Let me talk to Evan."

Jody rolled her eyes but passed him the cell phone.

Wilder's voice could be heard and Jody listened in. He was updating Evan on the site. Jody was a target. For a million. They already knew that. Wheezer had been working tirelessly to hack in and crack the account and dissolve the money, but he'd only made it through the first twelve layers of encryption. The account appeared to have many more. Time was running out.

Evan grunted, a hard expression on his face. "Okay. Time to switch gears then."

ELEVEN

Evan glanced at Jody. She was listening to every word Wilder said. He turned his back—not that it would help, but he'd noticed in the past few hours she was hanging by a thread. He wanted to shield her, protect her. Instead, he'd gotten her tossed onto a hit list. He shouldn't have climbed in that SUV with her but run the opposite direction into the woods and away from CCM. Away from her.

The only way to save her now was to do what he'd protested earlier. They'd have to fake their deaths. She'd never fake hers alone and leave him to run from the law without her, but that's what needed to happen.

He crushed the phone to his ear. "It's time to die. The both of us."

"What?" Jody belted and spun him around. "Now that I'm in the mix, you've changed your mind? I don't want to fake my death and lay low. I want to catch Lawman1."

Now she knew how he felt. But she was safer if they thought she was dead.

"Now is not the time to argue, Jo."

"Jody!" she insisted. Only because she was mad.

"Hey," Wilder said. "Something else you need to know before you two die to the world. Wheezer did some searching. Did you know Terry Pratt was stationed in the Philippines for two years?"

"No," Evan said. "But that's where the ghost gun suppliers are from."

"Yeah. He may have a personal connection and be in deeper than we originally suspected. How did he get on your task force? You choose him?"

"He asked and we're friends. We play in a weekly basketball league. He's a family guy."

"Well, did you know that in the past four months he paid off his house and bought a boat?"

Evan pinched the bridge of his nose. "I did know he bought a boat, but it's nothing fancy. Nothing that would raise a red flag." Didn't look good for Terry, though.

"Something else," Wilder said. "Wheezer found spyware on your phone. I'm guessing this Lawman1 used one of your inside agents—Terry Pratt is number one on my list—to get it on there."

The shock knocked Evan's breath from his

lungs. This meant Lawman1 had access to all of Evan's personal and private information, including his bank accounts and passwords he kept stored in his phone. That's how he could create an offshore account and make it appear like Evan had sent the message to Lawman1 ratting out his task force in return for money. The setup had been easy on Lawman1's part. Evan thought his encryptions on his own phone were foolproof. But this explained how he'd been tracked and duped. He could kick himself.

"I can't believe this."

"You weren't searching for it," Wilder said, "and Wheezer said it was deeply embedded. Top-shelf spyware. Not available to the average joe."

"What about the Suburban? Did you find a tracker or anything on it?"

"No, it was clean. But that only means someone could have removed it so there wouldn't be any evidence."

Evan shook his head and looked at the man still hiccupping through tears. "What exact information did the site give about our location? The park, or was it detailed coordinates?"

"The first time I looked, it said the park but to check back for more information later. I didn't get a chance to check again."

Jody's nose was scrunched the way it always was when she was in deep thought. Her eyes widened. "What do you carry on you at all times that would seem insignificant?" Jody asked. "Gun?"

"I'd have noticed something on my gun."

Jody frowned. "Check it anyway. If someone could get your phone, then they could get other items you keep with it. Like your gun."

Evan kept his gun in his drawer, locked with his phone and his... He dug into the backpack, into the waterproof bag and grabbed his wallet. He combed through it meticulously, and there, tucked deep into one of the credit card folds, was a tiny tracking chip.

Jody's lip curled. "That's how they're doing it. And it confirms once again someone in your office is working for the wrong side."

Evan destroyed the chip and tossed it.

"Who has access to your desk?" Jody asked.

"Anyone. Everyone. But I keep my drawer locked." Could have been picked though when he was in another office, the hall, at the coffee-pot. The magnitude of betrayal sent his gut into a spiral.

"Hey," Wilder said. "Meet us at the rendez-vous point—"

"Evan!" Jody was already running.

Grandpa Hitman was barreling through the woods. He must have used their small argument when they weren't paying attention to make a run for it.

"What's going on?" Wilder demanded.

"Nothing." He hollered for Jody to stop. "A loose cannon. We'll make the rendezvous point."

"She better be in one piece, Novak."

"She will be." He hung up, pocketed the phone and ran after Jody. "Jo!" He got her to stop about forty feet away. "Let him go." What were they going to do with him anyway?

"He tried to kill us. He might try again!"

Evan rested his hands on her shoulders. "No, he won't. He's not a cold-blooded killer. Besides, he left everything behind. I've got his phone. He isn't getting away, but for now he isn't our biggest issue. Killing ourselves is." And finding a way to prove Evan's innocence.

"Evan, just because we fake our deaths doesn't mean you can tuck me somewhere to hide while you go rogue, and it doesn't mean it will even work. Lawman1 is so far ahead of us, he might know it's a faked death!"

Evan had already thought of that. As much as he wanted Jody to go lay low somewhere, it might not be possible. And he wanted to protect her. To show her he could. To regain her trust. "I'm sticking by your side. I know I didn't in the past when it counted. But I'm not leaving again. I'll prove it to you." He prayed his words were true. Dad had asked for the same chances.

And failed.

But he had to try. Even if in the end it wouldn't change anything between them. Maybe…maybe they could part as friends. Although, he wasn't sure he could.

He wanted more.

Jody studied his face, then nodded. "Okay. Since we're being honest, I'm really worried. We're being hedged in on every side."

His insides shattered and he drew her to his chest and embraced her, caressing her hair. "It's going to be okay. We're going to fake our deaths, send the photos to Wheezer and let him upload them onto the site and receive the Bitcoin payment. We're going to make it to the rendezvous point, get somewhere safe and find out who Lawman1 is and bring down him and Terry Pratt. The truth will come out. We win. Besides, the Bible says we're hard-pressed on every side but not crushed." So far they weren't struck down.

They had to keep going. Keep fighting.

She burrowed against him and he relished her warmth. They'd made strides from the day of the convention. But that only made it harder to separate—for him to go his own way once they made it out of this.

"You make it sound easy. But none of this has been easy. Not physically—" she peered up at him "—not emotionally."

He ran his thumb across her high cheekbone, a smattering of dirt coming with him. "I know," he whispered. "One step at a time. We trust God.

Right?" She'd made a few strides with Him, too, hadn't she?

She nodded. "Right. Funny, I never thought I'd ever say that again and I sure never expected you to."

Evan chuckled. "Me, either."

Jody pointed at the dead squirrels hanging on the tree. "Let's use the crossbow." She crossed to the tent and claimed it. "Lay down. I'm gonna make it look like you took one to the chest. Then you can do the same with me." She scrunched her nose as she approached the squirrel.

"Of all the things I pictured us doing together, this is certainly not one of them." He lay down. "One day we'll look back and laugh as we reminisce. 'Hey, remember that time we faked our deaths in the woods?'"

"Real funny." She knelt over him, upper lip curled. "Hold still. Look deader than that."

When the deed was done and uploaded from the old man's phone to Wheezer, they set off on their trek to Wilder. Evan had to admit he felt more secure knowing Beckett Marsh wasn't far behind them, tracking them, being their eyes and ears. Jody explained he had excellent tracking skills.

"According to the compass, we should be about half a mile from the clearing. My thigh is on fire." Jody rubbed at it and winced.

The trees began to thin out and a clearing came into view.

Where was Wilder?

"Let's wait here until he lands. Trees can shield us."

"Good plan," Jody said, and leaned against the tree, resting her head on the trunk and closing her eyes. "I want to clean up and crawl in my bed. Nothing better than Egyptian cotton and a heated blanket. And a soft drink. I want a two-liter of anything carbonated and loaded with caffeine and sugar."

Evan chuckled. "I want loaded BBQ nachos with extra cheese and jalapeños and a pitcher of sweet tea."

A low whistle had Evan drawing his gun.

It came again.

"Get down."

"No." Jody grinned. "That's Beckett!" She whistled back, and the former navy SEAL popped out from behind a tree, dark hair curled around his brow and in full camouflage.

He gave a lopsided grin. "You left cold coffee for me back at that last site. You can apologize later," he teased.

They hadn't even drunk the coffee the old man had been brewing.

Jody hugged him. "It's good to see you."

He patted her back and shook Evan's hand. "You leave heavy boot marks."

Evan smiled. "With your tracking skills and Jody's smeller, no wonder you don't have dogs on your team."

Beckett laughed and Jody punched Evan.

For the moment there was hope.

Chopper blades whirred in the distance.

Wilder was on his way.

Hope soared. It rested in Evan's heart. On Jody's face.

"Who's ready to take a ride home?" Beckett asked as a sleek black chopper began its descent, tree branches wobbling from the commotion. Freezing air.

Evan clasped Jody's hand and they hauled it from the trees into the clearing. Running against resistance from the powerful wind from the chopper. Squinting against it, they barreled toward safety. The door was open and ready.

The noise deafening.

Hunching over as they came closer, Evan squeezed Jody's hand.

She squeezed back and smiled, then shock filled her face and she crumpled to the ground.

What happened? Had her leg given out?

Blood seeped through her pant leg. Too much blood.

She'd been hit and he hadn't even heard the shot because of the helicopter's blades.

Jody lay still, eyes closed. She'd passed out.

Her entire pant leg was turning crimson. Gunshot must have nicked an artery.

Wilder hollered, but Evan couldn't hear him with the heavy sound of the chopper blades and engine. Wilder returned cross fire into the woods.

Evan grabbed Jody up and ran for all he had toward the chopper. Beckett covered him from behind.

Oh, God! Please let her live. He'd promised Wilder he'd get her to him in one piece, but she'd been wounded. "Stay with me, Jo."

He powered his legs harder and ducked below the blades, jumping into the chopper. Blood continued to seep from the wound. Beckett bounded inside. "Go!"

Wilder turned, headset and dark sunglasses on. "Don't you let her die, Novak!"

Evan ripped the thigh of her pant leg open and blood spurted. Oh, no. "Get to a hospital, Wilder. Now!"

"Roger that!" The chopper lifted off and Wilder took them through the air while Evan applied pressure to Jody's wound. "Get me something to make a tourniquet. Wake up, Jo. I need you to wake up."

Beckett grabbed a medical kit, his mouth a grim line as he made a tourniquet. Evan tied it on.

"Jody, please wake up. We're losing her!" He couldn't lose her. She could not bleed out in this chopper before his very eyes.

Her eyes fluttered open.

"Evan," she barely whispered.

"I'm right here. Right here, Jo." He leaned down and kissed her softly.

"Don't…don't leave me." She held his gaze, but her pupils were dilated. Too dilated.

He leaned down to her ear. "I won't leave you. I'll stay by your side. I promise."

"Promise," she whispered again.

"Promise. I'm not going anywhere."

Her eyes shuttered.

"Wake up, Jo. Wake up!" His pulse ran at a dangerous speed. He looked at Beckett in a panic.

Beckett's eyes held a calm he needed. He breathed in. Out. Willed himself not to panic. Not to go berserk with the fact that he was unable to heal her. To save her. To protect her.

"How much longer, Wilder?" he called.

Below, Evan saw Atlanta come into view and the hospital helipad. Wilder radioed that he was making an emergency landing and told them Jody's condition.

What was her condition?

She'd turned white.

Her nails had a bluish tint.

"Starting CPR!"

* * *

"She's blessed to be alive…full recovery… rest…"

Muffled voices tickled Jody's ears. She was floating. Head fuzzy.

She'd been running for the helicopter when a searing pain had ripped through her leg, dropping her to the ground.

Bits and pieces came back to her.

Evan had carried her to the chopper.

Stayed with her.

I won't leave you. I'll stay by your side. I promise.

The promise had come through loud and clear and embedded like a treasure, shattering what was left of the wall she'd built, leaving it open to trust. To possibly love him again. There was no question she cared for him, deeply.

Jody had nearly died.

She needed Evan and he'd promised to be here. And he was. Right now, holding her hand. She felt the warmth; heard him speaking to the doctor or the nurse.

He'd proved he wouldn't abandon her.

What did this mean for them? Did it mean *he* might be open to love again? To give it a second chance?

Her lips felt like heavy towels soaked in water.

She could barely pry them apart. "How…how long have I been here?"

"Several hours. It was touch and go, kiddo."

Kiddo.

Kiddo?

Jody forced her eyes open and blinked as Wilder came into her vision. He was holding her hand. "Where's Evan?" Had he stepped out for coffee? Water?

Wilder cleared his throat. "He…left."

No. That couldn't be. He'd promised her. She had almost died and he…he'd *left* her? Again? When she needed him most? "Where? Why?" She tried to sit up. Wilder eased her back down.

"You were hit in the leg. Nicked a minor artery. They got the bullet. Doctor doesn't think there will be nerve damage. So let's focus on that right now." Wilder's green eyes held a don't-fight-with-me glare. "I had to call your mama, but she knows she can't come, which is killing her. And I called Locke. Because for a minute, I didn't know, Jode. I didn't know."

Jody fought back tears. "Where did he go?"

"Wheezer uploaded the photos and the hit looks to be called off, finally. Lawman1 transferred the Bitcoin into an online wallet Wheezer set up, which we'll turn over to the authorities in good time. Now, let's hope all those gunning for you got the memo."

Agreed. "Where did Evan go? Mexico? Did he tell you?"

"He needs to know if Terry Pratt is the corrupt agent. He's decided to catch him dead to rights. He called him and asked for help laying low from the law until he can prove his innocence. If Terry is the corrupt agent, he's probably already informed Lawman1 and he'll know the deaths were faked—at least Evan's, but he'll suspect yours, as well. I doubt he'll put another hit on either of you, though, because that clearly gives away Terry. But we can't be sure of anything." He patted the bed railing. "I'm on 24/7 care of you until we do."

"Why would you let him do that, Wilder?" Jody tried to sit up again. It was painful but she pushed past it.

"I didn't let him. He was already on the phone with Terry when I found him and told him you were out of surgery."

"He didn't call from the hospital, did he?"

"I gave him a burner in case your escapee in the woods lets someone nefarious know you have his phone. I don't need anyone tracing it here and finding you."

"I don't, either."

"Terry told him he has a place he can stay on the DL until Evan can figure out who is framing him. I'd say that's where he is now."

Jody pushed back tears. Of hurt. Anger. If

Terry was working with Lawman1, then the safe location would be compromised and Evan was alone. With nothing but his Sig Sauer and a couple of bullets. What a stupid idea! "Did you give him a weapon?"

"Do I look like this might be my first dance? I'd have gone with him, but I needed to be here with you."

But Evan could leave her. Did.

"Beckett could have stayed with me or Shepherd."

"Shep had another assignment and Beckett has been awake for forty-eight hours straight. He's no good to anyone right now. Besides, *I'm* going to be here. Watch over you. I should have protected you better, kiddo."

"Don't even, Wilder." Leave it to him to take full responsibility for something he couldn't control. None of them had any control. "How long ago did Evan leave?"

"Hour or two maybe?"

Jody closed her eyes. "How far away is this so-called safe place?"

"'Bout thirty minutes from here."

She shook her head. "Get me out of here."

Wilder laughed but sobered quickly when she tried to get up.

She wasn't staying one more minute in this place. "Get me some meds and let's move."

"You just had surgery! You aren't going anywhere for forty-eight hours."

"Watch. Me." She wasn't going to let Evan go it alone. That was the difference between them. She followed through no matter what. She struggled for strength to swing her feet over the side of the hospital bed. Wilder reached over and pressed her pain pump.

Jody stared in horror. "What…what did you… do…?" Her eyes drooped as the meds hit her system fast. "I will…get…you for…this."

"Mmm-hmm. Night-night, kiddo."

Her last protests died on her lips as sleep overtook her.

Can't…breathe!

Jody's eyes popped open to darkness; something soft pressed against her face was suffocating her. Was she dreaming?

No!

She was being smothered in her hospital bed. Where was Wilder? Where was Evan?

Evan was gone. Left.

She used her right hand and gripped a slender but strong arm, gouging her nails into the thin, long-sleeved shirt her attacker wore. Jody couldn't be sure if it was a male or female.

Monitors beeped wildly.

She thrashed her head to wiggle out from

under the pillow. Trying to scream would give up too much precious oxygen and be too muffled.

Need to breathe.

She was about to lose consciousness…could feel it… No!

"She's asleep. I'll call if anything changes."

Wilder's voice!

Suddenly the pressure eased up and she shoved the pillow away. Her vision focused as she caught a woman in scrubs rushing from the room. She must have heard Wilder coming back, too.

He entered the room, phone in hand as Jody gasped for air and tried to hobble from the bed.

"What do you think you're doing?" Wilder barked. "I told you—"

"I was attacked!" Already she was removing the needle in her arm that linked to her IV.

Wilder whipped his head around the room and out into the hallway. "You're dreaming. A nurse just left."

"Well, she wasn't!" Jody screamed, and found her footing. Cold feet on the even colder tiled floor. She couldn't put much support on her leg.

"Stay here." Wilder sprinted from the room. All the nurses had scrubs. He'd never find her.

One thing was certain. Terry Pratt was a traitor. The only way a killer would know that Jody was here was if Terry had told Lawman1, who'd arranged to have Jody clipped, or if Terry himself had someone do it. Evan had compromised Jody's safety knowing she was vulnerable. Doped up. He couldn't have waited until she was released from the hospital to call Terry? Did he have to play the hero so soon?

Her blood raced hot. But as angry as she might be at Evan, as disappointed once again, she didn't want him dead, and she knew he wouldn't intentionally endanger her. But he wasn't thinking about her. He was thinking about him. Again. She'd seen a change in him. Trusted him.

And once more she'd been hurt.

Wilder entered the room. "Whoever it was got away and my hands are tied asking for help. It's out there, though, that you're here."

"Which is why I need to get out. They'll keep pumping me full of pain meds that make me groggy and you can't sit here 24/7. You might need to go to the bathroom!"

Wilder heaved a sigh. "As much as I hate to say it, you're right."

Another attempt to kill her would come, and she wasn't functioning on all cylinders. The overwhelming sense of helplessness swept over her and fear clutched at her chest, but she had to buck up. Pull it together. Fight.

"That was Evan on the phone, calling to check up on you."

How nice of him to check in on her. She bit down on the sarcastic thought. She refused to let old bitterness rise to the surface simply because she was hurt again. This time she'd take it to God. Lean on Him for support. *God, I'm so upset with Evan and mad at myself for falling for him again. For trusting him with my heart. Help me overcome it. I don't want to feel like I did all those years before.*

"He put me in jeopardy. Told Terry I was alive, too. Probably banking on the fact that you'd be here to protect me if someone came. And you did. I was passing out, Wilder. If you hadn't come…" She shuddered. "But we can't let that matter right now. We have to find him. He's next if they haven't already descended on that fake safe house."

Wilder pointed to a denim bag. "Cosette brought you a fresh bag with toiletries. I'll be outside."

Jody held her arm up and pointed to the small bruised area where the needle had administered pain meds. "You still got a whuppin' coming for that pain pump."

Wilder snorted. "The meds have made you delusional. Settle down, Feisty McFeister." He closed the door, leaving her alone with her thoughts.

Faking their deaths hadn't worked. Evan had told the bad guys they were alive by baiting Terry Pratt to see if he was the corrupt agent!

They weren't safe.

She didn't have all her strength.

Swallowing down a surge of panic and fear, she hoped they weren't too late to save Evan.

TWELVE

Evan sat in a recliner that smelled like mothballs. According to Terry, the 1500-square-foot home had belonged to his great-aunt, who had been moved into a nursing home a few months ago.

When he'd called Terry, he'd seemed relieved and grateful to hear Evan was alive and had even offered to give Evan a ride from his location to the house, but Evan couldn't give him that location because it would endanger Jody. A gnawing in his gut wouldn't let up. He'd promised her he'd be right by her side and not leave, and he hadn't—not until he knew she was going to pull through surgery. Then she'd need to sleep awhile in recovery. With her being so vulnerable, he needed to be proactive. Move fast. Take Terry down if he was the mole inside the agency and put the screws to him to find Lawman1 and arrest him.

Her safety meant everything to him. This

was the only way he could protect her. Wilder wouldn't let anything happen, so he'd felt safe to leave. Hopefully, in the next few hours he'd know if Terry was dirty or not, and he could get back to Jody.

But what did that mean? *Don't leave me.* Had Jody meant in the state she'd been in or…ever?

Was he doomed to repeat his father's mistakes or could he overcome them? If Jody could forgive him and even love him again, then surely he could find a way to break free from what history and his DNA told him he was.

There was no doubt he loved her. Had always loved her. Now, with God's help he might be able to love her better. Treat her like she should've been treated all along. Follow God's ways. She deserved so much more than what she'd been left with. But how could he continue to move up in the agency if he was with her? The guilt alone would eat away at him like acid. She might end up resenting him.

Even if he overcame all his private obstacles, that barrier still lay between them like an abyss. All he'd ever wanted was to serve and protect. To put away criminals. Every bad guy he caught and brought to justice was like defeating Dad over and over. Working in the Secret Service had garnered him respect and admiration.

But all he really wanted now was Jody's. And he wanted to keep it. Could he do that and take the promotion to Assistant Director of Protective Operations he was pretty much guaranteed if he brought these criminals down? He laughed. He was already giving himself a promotion and at this moment in time he was a fugitive!

Evan had to prove his innocence. Bring down Terry first. It crushed him to know his friend had done this to him, but he'd had access to pick the lock on Evan's desk drawer. He'd been in the Philippines. Asked to be on the task force. Paid off his house and bought a new boat in the past four months.

The old refrigerator hummed and the heat kicked off and on. The TV was on a local station—no DirecTV and definitely no high-def. Didn't matter. Evan couldn't concentrate on whatever was airing. He had no way to work online. No way to find out if Terry had gone to Lawman1 with the news Evan was alive and here. Terry would have no fear of getting caught because he'd trust Evan would be dead and unable to prove Terry's involvement. Wheezer hadn't called to say if the hit had been reinstated or not, but maybe they'd be more careful now and put out a private hit without using the dark web. The possibilities were endless.

As Evan turned off the TV, a shadow outside the window caught his eye. He grabbed his Sig Sauer and quietly edged to the living room, peeping through the curtain. A man dressed in black was stalking along the privacy fence, gun in hand.

Terry, how could you?

Evan moved through the house to the back door, where the intruder was probably going to make his entrance. Standing there, he had a straight view into the master bedroom.

The window was open.

Evan hadn't opened it.

Someone was already inside.

The intruder had to be in the bedroom. Evan would have spotted him in the kitchen. The other two small bedrooms were at the front of the house.

What was he waiting on?

Carefully and quietly, Evan slid a kitchen chair in front of the back door. If anyone entered, he'd hear the chair scrape across the tile. He crept into the bedroom. Dresser on the right. Bed in the center.

He toed the door back.

Resistance.

Adrenaline rushed at the same time the attacker did.

He shoved Evan into the dresser, the mirror shaking. The intruder grabbed Evan's wrist and slammed it against the wall, working to release his grip on the gun. Evan kneed the attacker in the gut and shoved him backward. He toppled onto the floor as the back door burst open, the wooden chair crashing onto the tile.

A second intruder pounced on Evan, slamming his fist into his cheek. The warmth of blood filled his mouth. He reached for the gun he'd dropped and the other attacker kicked it away, pointed his gun at Evan's head.

Evan grabbed the attacker from the back door and used him as a shield.

"Evan!"

Jody?

"Novak!"

Wilder?

"They have guns!" Evan hollered.

The armed attacker hurdled the bed and bolted through the window. The second attacker went for the same route, but Evan grabbed his ankle, pulling him down and cracking his jaw.

Jody entered the room, gun in her right hand, looking exhausted and pale. What was she doing here? She wasn't supposed to be released from the hospital yet.

Wilder entered behind her.

Evan kept the assailant pinned to the floor while Jody kept her aim on him. "Take his mask off. Let's see this slimeball."

He hesitated. So many questions right now. Like why was Jody here? And why wouldn't she look directly at him? Evan peeled off the mask to reveal a total stranger. "You trying to earn that two mil?" Evan asked.

His dark eyes held contempt, but behind it was surprise. Earning a fee for Evan's death was news to him. "I don't know nothing."

The guy couldn't be over twenty-five. A decent-looking kid, but hardened from life. His breath smelled of whiskey. A scar ran across his bottom lip. "Who hired you to kill me?"

"I don't know nothing."

"Which means you know something or you missed English class, my friend," Wilder said, and stepped forward, a dark strand of black hair falling in his eyes. He squatted and placed the barrel of the gun between the boy's eyes. "That's a double negative. Either way, I don't care." He pressed it in, sending the attacker into a panic-laced spasm. "Name and who hired you to come here."

"No one hired me."

Wilder's eyes narrowed and he slid the barrel of the gun onto the tip of the guy's nose. "You don't give me the answer I'm after, I won't think twice about puttin' a slug right through your snot-box." Even Evan wasn't sure if Wilder was serious or not. The man clearly knew how to be scary, but then, he'd been a SEAL.

Evan grabbed the attacker's shirt and gave him a good shake.

"Okay...but... I'm dead either way." His voice

came out nasally from Wilder's gun still pressing into his nose.

"Name? Who do you work for?" Evan asked.

"Jose Rodriguez, and I work for Robert Ramos."

Evan shook his head. Name didn't ring a bell. "Why are you here?"

The attacker went cross-eyed as he stared at the gun on his nose. Evan motioned for Wilder to let up. He complied and the man gritted his teeth. "What kind of deal am I going to get? I need witness protection or something!"

They couldn't make deals, but they didn't have time to make the necessary calls. Besides, this guy might be blowing smoke. Evan read him his rights. He wanted this to go down properly. "Tell us what you know and we'll see what we can do."

"Robert Ramos runs guns. From the Philippines."

"Ghost guns," Evan said.

"Yeah. He got wind he'd made a deal with the Law. That you—" he looked directly at Evan "—were running some kind of task force to take Ramos and his business down."

"By who?" Evan asked.

"I don't know. Above my pay grade. I do what I'm told and I was told to come here and eliminate you."

"By Ramos himself? Or someone else?"

"David Knightly. Works for Ramos. And

once Mario gets back to him and tells him I was caught, I'll be dead."

Evan filed the names away. Mario was the attacker who got away. David Knightly was a middle man for the guy Evan had been trying to bring down— Robert Ramos. But without either one of them in custody to interrogate, Evan wasn't sure if Lawman1 had spilled it to Ramos or if Terry Pratt had done it himself. Either way, they had to be working in tandem.

Jody limped forward. "Do you know who attacked me at the hospital today?"

What? Evan snapped his head in Jody's direction. Jody had been attacked? Rage coursed through his veins and he tightened his grip on this guy's shirt, but the real rage he directed toward himself.

Evan hadn't been there like he'd said he would.

No wonder she wore such a cool expression.

He'd made her a promise.

And he'd broken it.

He could hardly breathe. He was his dad. There was no overcoming it.

Why had he made that *stupid* move?

"I asked about my attack," Jody said.

"No! I don't know nothing about that. I promise!" Jose shook his head like a dog on a bone.

Evan jerked him up and to his feet. He wasn't sure who to call to have this idiot carted off and further questioned. He was a fugitive and couldn't reveal his whereabouts. Terry was a traitor. "Were you at the junkyard when the deal went south?"

"Maybe."

That was a yes.

Wilder pulled his phone. "I have a local FBI friend. August Fenner. I'll have him here to deal with this moron." Wilder hit a button on his phone. "Hey, August, how ya doing?… Cashing in a favor, bud… As a matter of fact it *will* require discretion." He tossed Evan a pair of cuffs and exited the room.

Evan cuffed Jose and peeked at Jody, shame begging him to turn away, but he had to know, had to see into those blue eyes. "What happened to you today?"

Instantly he regretted it. If looks could melt a person, Evan would be a puddle of goo right now.

"I woke up to a pillow over my face."

"That was not me!" Jose insisted.

"Shut up!" Evan bellowed. He waited for Jody to continue. He should have been there. "And?"

"And I decided on an early checkout." She remained tight-lipped. Cool. If Evan reached out, he was certain he'd be able to touch a tangible wall she'd erected between them. A wall that had crumbled in the few short days they'd been together.

This time it felt impenetrable.

He had no one to blame but himself. Now

wasn't the time to press further. "We have to find Terry."

"Oh, I know," Jody said, laying on heavy condescension, eyes narrowed but hazy from the pain meds. "That's your priority. Getting cleared. Getting your honorable reputation back and making sure your precious name and identity isn't tarnished."

Evan couldn't breathe.

He did want all those things but not more than he wanted her to be safe, but his actions weren't declaring that. All she saw was another promise broken. He'd made a choice to leave hoping to protect her and he'd failed in every sense of the word.

What could he say? Sorry?

She wouldn't believe him. The past was there to affirm it.

Evan had stopped believing Dad's apologies, too, even when he had seen desperation in his eyes. There wasn't a thing he could say or do and certainly not here in front of this thug.

His lungs turned to iron.

His head spun.

How could he make this right? If there was any way at all.

"Jody, I meant Terry Pratt has proved he's our guy. He knows you're alive."

Jody's jaw dropped. "My suspicion was right. You left me *and* used me as bait knowing I was

drugged up and not at my best! I trusted you—"
She glanced at Jose and held her tongue.

She'd finally given him her trust and he'd
blown it. Panic gripped him. "That is not what
happened. I—"

"August will be here in five." Wilder popped
back in the room but slid a glance from Jody to
Evan. The tension was palpable. "So...he knows
everything, Evan, and he's willing to risk some
things for me...for you. We can trust him."

Evan didn't ask questions. His head was spin-
ning.

Wilder frowned.

"Why didn't you tell me she'd been attacked
when we were on the phone earlier?" Evan asked.

"Because it happened while I was on the
phone with you." Wilder eyed Jody. "You told
him everything?"

"She did not." Evan worked his jaw. What was
everything?

"I'm fine," Jody said, and stormed from the
room—best someone could with a bum leg.

Wilder's eyes gave the truth away.

It hadn't just been an attack. It had been a serious close call.

A knock came.

FBI.

Jody sipped a cup of hot tea in the CCM
kitchen. Two days had passed since Jose Ro-

driguez had been taken in and questioned by the FBI. Special Agent Fenner must really owe Wilder a big one—one that could jeopardize his own career. Basically, he was aiding and abetting fugitives for Wilder, but he'd been a SEAL with him, so there was some kind of brotherhood and loyalty that ran thicker than blood.

None of which Evan would know about.

Except deep within, Jody knew that wasn't true. He was loyal to the Secret Service and he'd never been unfaithful to her during all their dating years. At the moment, she was nursing a tender heart. Questioning herself. Evan.

They'd lain low at CCM. It was an iffy move, but with the kind of surveillance they had around the property, they'd know if law enforcement was descending or camping out, spying. They'd see a drone. Hear a chopper. But Terry Pratt knew Evan was in Atlanta—somewhere. Jody doubted he'd tell his supervisor that information—whether he was a good guy or bad, it could land him in prison. He'd also aided and abetted a fugitive regardless of his motives.

Evan hadn't taken off to Mexico. That was a surprise, but now that he had Jose and was convinced Terry Pratt was the dirty agent, he'd want to stick close. Catch his man. Jody felt the bitterness and prayed that God would help her work through the feelings that cropped up unwanted.

Evan should catch his man. They'd stripped

him of everything he held dear. He was on the run but innocent. She shouldn't fault him for doing everything in his power as quickly as possible to right this injustice.

But her heart didn't think logically—it shouted that he'd abandoned her again and broken a promise.

She limped to the kitchen to pour another cup of tea.

Citrus and cinnamon.

The last forty-eight hours, Jody had secluded herself in her apartment. In part because she didn't want to see Evan. But she needed the rest and recovery time. Evan had either respected that or didn't have the words to apologize to make things right.

But here he was now.

"I want to talk to you." He spoke softly, a hint of uncertainty in his voice.

"About what?" Jody kept her eyes on the electric teakettle.

"What happened in the hospital. I would never use you as bait. I never told Terry you were there. I was trying to protect you."

She spun around. "Fat lot of good that did."

Evan pinched the bridge of his nose. "I regret the choice I made, Jody. I should have stayed."

Jody refused to cry, to cave. She couldn't take any more pain and suffering in the name of Evan Novak. She needed a clean break. For good. "You promised you'd stay. Would one more hour or two…a day have killed you?"

"No." He hung his head.

Jody set her cup of tea on the counter. "I'm not sorry for forgiving you. I needed it for myself. But I am sorry I trusted you again." Everything was shattering inside. She swallowed the growing lump burning her throat. "I'll see you to the end. Like I promised. Then that's it, Evan."

Evan's nostrils flared and his jaw twitched. "I did it for you."

Evan's need to be everything his father wasn't had him bound. His desire to show he was a man of honor, good reputation and respect in the public eye had destroyed everything in his personal life. Anger passed and nothing was left but loss and regret and pity.

"No," she murmured, "you did it for you." She faced him. "You didn't have to show yourself a hero by leaving me to take down a bad guy. Staying by my side would have proved that." Tears pooled in her eyes against her will. "You're the only man I've ever loved. And you're the only one who's broken my heart. Repeatedly. I'm such an idiot. I thought that maybe the new you and me could be something again, even after everything that happened between us."

"Jody—"

She squeezed her eyes shut. "I needed you again. And you let me believe I had you. I don't think I've *ever* had you, Evan." She strangled a cry and tried to blink away the hot tears.

"That's not true," he whispered.

"You never committed to me."

"I did. I was always faithful to you," he pleaded.

"You wouldn't even marry me." She inhaled sharply. "And I'm done. I have to be done. For good. Forever."

The sharp lines of his Adam's apple bobbed with his swallow. A sheen filmed his eyes, but he studied her, searching for truth. *Look closely, Evan. I mean it.*

Pain flickered across his face when it became apparent he'd recognized she meant every word, as much as it hurt to say it. He gave a resolute nod. "Jo, you're the only woman *I've* ever loved—the only woman I'll ever love. But I've done it badly." He raked a hand through his hair. "And I *am* sorry. But you're right. I have hurt you repeatedly and—"

Wilder burst into the kitchen with Cosette hot on his heels. Looked like they'd been in some kind of argument again. "I need coffee and I have news."

"Wilder Flynn!" Cosette stood with her hands on her hips, red lips pursed.

"Nope." He swung open a cabinet door and yanked out a mug. "Go away."

Cosette's face turned as cherry as her lips. "Everyone on our team includes you. It's important."

"I'm busy." Wilder poured a cup and drank it deep and black. "Jose Rodriguez cut a deal with the DA and offered up Robert Ramos. His assets have been frozen. FBI analysts are working through his accounts now. Warrant is out for Ramos's arrest."

Evan frowned. "I want access to those accounts, too."

"Had a feeling you'd say that." He raised his mug to Cosette. "I'm the boss. End of discussion." He and Evan waltzed out of the kitchen, and Cosette went to blabbering in Cajun French and stormed out behind them.

Lord, Evan didn't fight for me. Not then. Not now.

He'd agreed without an explanation.

Never even responded to her statement about marriage.

But this time she would trust God. For healing. For renewed hope. For strength.

An hour later, Jody entered Wheezer's office. Organized chaos. Wilder and Evan loomed over him.

"What's going on?" she asked.

"Agent Fenner called. Ramos is in custody. He's not talking—may never—but his hard drives are telling some of the tale," Evan said. "I need to know who Terry Pratt notified about me being alive and in the safe house."

"How long until you'll know anything?" Jody

asked, trying not to make too much eye contact with Evan.

"We set up the gun trade two weeks ago, so they'll make that time frame a priority. See if there are any emails between Terry Pratt and Ramos—or Lawman1 and Ramos. Of course this all depends on whether or not they were making their emails untraceable."

Seemed like they were hunting a needle in a haystack. "What about phone records? They subpoena those, too?" Jody eased onto the black leather sofa, her leg throbbing and needing a break.

Evan nodded. "They'll be looking—"

Wilder's phone rang. "Hello." He listened for a few moments and grinned. "Thanks." He hung up. "Ramos used his private email and we have who informed him of the gun deal sting. It was Lawman1."

Evan frowned. "We only have Ramos's emails. He might have been stupid enough to use his private email with no encryption, but you can bank that Lawman1 did. They won't be able to trace his IP address."

Jody propped her leg up and winced. "Well, we know Lawman1 was told first, and while it could be anyone on your task force, Pratt only knew that we were alive…and our locations."

"I didn't tell him, Jody." Evan rubbed the back of his neck. "I knew revealing I was alive would make me a bull's-eye, but I'd never endanger you."

Wilder looked at his phone and groaned, then narrowed his eyes. "I think it was me."

"You?"

Glancing at Evan, he said, "When I told you that Jode was out of surgery, you were on the phone. With Terry. He must have overheard."

Evan perched on the edge of the desk. "That's the only way he could know."

Earlier in the woods, Jody had heard everything Wilder had said when Evan was on the cell phone with him. It wasn't far-fetched.

Wilder's fist balled. "I should have been more careful. I'm sorry, kiddo."

Well, at least Evan hadn't offered her up as bait. Didn't change anything, though. So far all they had on Terry was circumstantial. They needed hard proof, but Evan couldn't do anything that might be inadmissible in court.

Their hands were tied.

Unless…

"How about we confront Terry. He doesn't have to know we don't have anything concrete. Evan, if anyone can make him believe evidence has been mined from the cyber world, it's you. We can get him to cough up who Lawman1 really is, and if he doesn't know, we use him to draw Lawman1 out."

Evan rubbed his hands over his face. Exhaustion was making its mark. "We can try. His safe house was breached. That alone might make him squirm since I'm not dead. I'm sure he's been notified that the FBI descended on his aunt's house and an arrest was made. We can use it."

"And I'm going." She pointed to her leg. "He owes it to my face as much as he does yours."

Evan didn't argue. "You can come, but you can't drive." He smiled but sorrow couldn't be hidden in his eyes.

He helped her to the car, and once he was inside she shifted and swallowed her pride. "I'm sorry."

Evan glanced at her. "For what?"

"Accusing you of using me as bait."

"Apology accepted. Can't blame you for thinking the worst of me. I've done the worst to you."

She kept silent for fear her voice might crack. Instead, she clicked her seat belt in place and hoped they could get Terry Pratt to confess.

THIRTEEN

Evan white-knuckled the steering wheel, unfocused. He should have come clean and told Jody he'd never proposed because he was a coward—afraid he'd wreck their marriage and it would end in divorce like Mom and Dad's. Better not to marry her and not end up like Dad than to marry her and watch the train wreck happen, unable to control it. She would have tried to convince him otherwise if he'd confessed that truth back then. She wouldn't have understood. She had no idea what it was like to live with this fear. This doom hanging over his head.

And he'd loved her so much he might have let her convince him—for a while.

Until he became the man who hurt the woman he loved. *Repeatedly.* That had been her exact word.

Well, he wouldn't give himself the chance to do it again. Once justice was served to Terry Pratt and Lawman1, Evan would disappear from

Jody's life and all the pain he inflicted by being in it.

But he felt like any moment he might implode and he'd crumple on the pavement. Walking away was the right thing. The selfless thing. The sacrificial thing. The only way he knew he could love her and protect her.

She believed he'd left the hospital to be the hero to his colleagues, to the public. And his actions said as much. But he'd wanted her safe. Fast.

Evan's words were worthless.

His actions had failed.

Evan tried to be the man of God the Bible said he could be. He failed daily. But he wanted to be the kind of man Jody could be proud of, even if only he would know it. She was done with him.

He turned into Terry Pratt's driveway.

"Well…here goes everything." He stepped out of the SUV and winced as Jody struggled to climb out. Wounded because of his mess up.

He knocked on Terry's door.

Michael Pratt opened it. "Hey, man." He glanced at Jody and back to Evan. "I heard you were on the run. It was all over the news."

"Long story. Your dad here?" His car wasn't in the drive.

"We were sitting down to a pizza. You hungry?"

"No, thanks," Evan answered, and they followed Michael inside.

Terry entered the room. "Bro! Shouldn't you be laying low at the safe house? Anyone finds you here, we're both in trouble."

Evan folded his arms and Jody stared Terry down.

"What's going on?" Terry asked cautiously.

"You tell us," Evan said, and updated him on what had happened at the hospital and the safe house. As if he didn't already know. "Who is Lawman1?"

Terry's eyes widened and he tossed his hands up. "I have no idea. I put my backside on the line to help you. I didn't tell anyone you called."

"You're the only one I told. We have Robert Ramos in custody."

Terry frowned. "Who's Robert Ramos?"

"The ghost gun dealer. Why didn't you tell me you were stationed in the Philippines?"

"I thought you knew. Why else would I want a piece of the action taking these guys down? I saw what those guns did."

"How did you pay off your house and buy a boat on your salary?"

Terry stepped forward. "I didn't tip off Lawman1 about the deal that night. I never did anything, and how I spend money is none of your business."

"Then I'd like to see your private laptop and your phone." Evan wanted to see if he had the anonymous browser downloaded. Wanted to see his texts.

"No. You can take my word, or take yourself out of my house right now." The vein in his neck popped and his face flushed red.

If he had nothing to hide why not let Evan probe his computer?

Jody seemed confused about something. Distracted.

"Maybe the DA can cut you a deal, too, Terry."

"I don't need a deal. I haven't done anything."

Evan laughed humorlessly. "I have no devices left. No tracking chips. Nothing. The only thing left is you. Why do you think I even called?"

"I hope because you trusted me!" He pointed to the front door.

"If you trust me give me your personal laptop. Give me your phone. Don't make me get a warrant. I promise one is coming."

"Dad?" Michael came into the room. "What's going on? I think you need to leave, Evan."

"Give me the phone and laptop."

"No."

"I'm coming for you, Terry." He spun on his heel and followed Jody out the door. "He's guilty and I can't prove it."

"I know. But you will."

The door opened and Terry flagged him down. "Wait! Wait, Evan."

Evan paused at the door. "You want to confess?"

"Yeah." He hung his head. "I do." He closed the distance. "But not to being corrupt. I never made a deal with anyone. I love my job."

"Then what are you going to confess?"

Jody climbed out of the SUV.

Terry glanced back toward the house. "Michael gambles. More than he should and he's lost a lot. I covered some of his debt with credit cards. He won pretty big not long ago and he repaid me by paying off the house and buying me the boat."

"Anything else?"

"I'll give you my laptop." He handed Evan his phone. "And this." He walked to his car next to Jody and opened it.

Her eyes grew wide. "How long have you been having an affair?" she asked.

Evan snapped his attention toward her. "What?"

"I smell the perfume. The car reeks of it. That and extra pine freshener to mask it. It's not his wife's perfume. I smelled hers in the house but also another scent on you. Most women stick with one fragrance." She sniffed again. "You want to tell him with who or do you want me to?"

Evan's head spun. Terry had been married twenty-eight years. They were happy. Weren't they? "Terry?"

Shame drooped his shoulders. "It just happened."

"Affairs do not just happen," Evan said.

"I've been seeing Layla. About six months."

Layla? His investigative support assistant? "She's young enough to be your daughter! She's a year younger than Michael!" Not that age mattered. The affair was wrong no matter how old Layla was, but still… "Are you having some kind of midlife crisis?"

"I don't know!" Terry wailed.

She'd been coming to see the games because of Terry and dragging Zoey so it wouldn't look suspicious. "Is that why you didn't want to give me the laptop and phone?"

Terry nodded. "There are texts and emails between us. But you won't find anything else because I did not cross you or the team."

Layla.

You left your phone on your desk and it's been beeping for five minutes.

He'd been out of sorts and forgotten to lock it up. With her tech savviness, she could have easily downloaded spyware. And she could have picked the lock on his drawer and placed the tracking chip in his wallet.

"Did you tell Layla I called you and told you I was alive? Did she overhear about Jody? Did *you*?" Evan asked.

She had access to his files. His computer. The task force information, including all their usernames, *She* could be working with Lawman1. She might even know him personally.

Michael stepped outside. "Dad? Everything okay?"

"Go back inside, son. It's fine." He turned to Evan and lowered his voice. "I did overhear about Jody, but you hung up so fast I never got to ask about her. Layla isn't involved."

"Did you tell her, though?"

"No." Terry bit his bottom lip. "But she was next to me when you called."

She could easily have overheard.

"Bro," Terry said. "She's been worried and asking about you nonstop. It's not her."

What if SAC Bevin did believe in Evan's innocence and it wasn't a ruse? What if Layla wanted to keep him on the run so the killers would eventually hit their target?

"I'm going to run an analysis on these devices." Evan handed them off to Jody and she put them in the SUV. "Don't leave the state."

"I'm not guilty of anything except betraying my marriage."

And if he'd betray the woman he'd pledged his life to, he would certainly betray Evan. "Tell no one about this visit. I'll be in touch." Evan climbed inside his SUV. Michael peered through the window.

Now to see what Terry's computer and phone turned up.

* * *

Jody yawned and brewed a second pot of coffee. It had only been twenty-four hours since they'd talked to Terry. They hadn't been able to locate Layla and she wouldn't answer her phone or texts. Evan had been holed up with Wheezer on a computer while Jody had worked other angles and was forced by Wilder and Cosette to take it easy.

They had found out that Robert Ramos did not know Lawman1 personally. It appeared no one did. Evan had combed through Terry's devices and, while there were many romantic emails and texts between him and Layla, there was nothing that proved they'd conspired against Evan and Jody. But there were ways to stay hidden, and they didn't have enough probable cause to get warrants served to search homes and personal property.

The coffeepot beeped as someone knocked on her apartment door. She hobbled to answer it. Evan stood before her, freshly showered. A hint of coffee lingered on him.

"Any news?" she asked.

"Wheezer found a way to prove I didn't set up that offshore account. I'd tell you the technical part, but you'd go cross-eyed. It was genius, though, and I didn't think of it."

"That's great. You'll be exonerated and able

to go back into work. No more running from the good guys." Just the bad ones.

"Yeah. But that's not all. Wheezer overrode the encryption using a program he wrote and he cracked open an IP address from an internet café in Florida. I clearly was not in Florida so it couldn't have been me." He grinned. "You're right. It would be terrifying if Wheezer worked for the opposite side of the law."

"Are you saying Lawman1 sent the fake email from you to himself from Florida or made it appear to be from there?"

"It came directly from Florida. Wilder has a friend in Turtle Bay—Tom Kensington. He's not far from where the email was sent. He's going to check out the café and ask around. See if there are any regulars in there. We're a step closer."

"Good. I'm glad to hear that."

"And that money in the offshore account? It's actually empty, but Lawman1 hacked the banking system to make it appear that funds were in the account."

"Could he have done that with the assassination site?"

"Probably. But he didn't. That Bitcoin is legit in the online wallet Wheezer set up, which will go to proper authorities now that all charges have been dropped and I'm no longer a fugitive. Agent Fenner sent the information to my supervising agent. Clive called the CCM office and I talked to him about ten minutes ago. He wants me to come in for a briefing and reinstatement."

Jody leaned on the door frame. She wasn't angry that Evan had his life back, his job. His reputation. He'd worked hard and deserved it. "That must be a relief."

"It is." His relaxed expression suddenly shifted as if some new revelation had dawned on him.

"What is it?"

He blinked and pursed his lips.

"Evan? What's wrong?"

"I—uh… Nothing." He cleared his throat. "SAC Bevin asked me why I never came in after he emailed me. He did believe me. Which means…"

"Layla was lying about it being a ruse. She wanted you to stay on the run."

Evan called her cell phone again. Voice mail. He tried the office. A few moments later he hung up. "She's not in the office today, either."

That didn't sound good. "You think she ran for it? What about Terry?"

"He's been into work. If he's innocent, why not, right?" He snapped his fingers. "I know someone who might know where Layla is." He called Zoey, spoke for a moment and then hung up. "She says Layla is spending a few days with her mama, who lives outside Atlanta. Apparently, she's 'going through some stuff' and needed some time."

"I imagine she is. Let's get Wheezer to find her mama's address."

"Good idea." A few texts later, Evan had it. "You feel up to going for a ride? Sniff her out. Not literally of course." He chuckled under his breath.

"It's worth the drive to see if she's there. If not, maybe her mom knows where she might be." Jody grabbed her coat and followed Evan to the Suburban.

Thirty minutes into the drive, Evan's phone rang. "Wilder." He put the phone on speaker.

"Hey, it's Wheezer."

"And Wilder."

"Go ahead, you're on speaker," Evan said.

"I have some news," Wheezer said. "I tried a new approach to looking at the way that offshore account was set up."

"Spare us all the nerd knowledge, Wheezer, and give us the short version," Jody said. She glanced at Evan. "Sorry, but it all makes my head hurt." Who cared about the how when they might have a why and a who.

Evan grinned. "Bottom line then."

Wheezer continued, "I found a way into the Florida internet café's mainframe and used it to find another IP address that linked to the one we found earlier. I used that to get us a physical location."

Great news. "And?" Jody asked.

Wilder spoke. "It's a residence about fifteen miles from the café. Owned by Roger and Marsha Vanhatter."

Excitement raced through Jody's veins. "Are you saying you found Lawman1 and his real identity?"

"They don't fit the bill. But Wheezer searched around and discovered they have a daughter and son both in their early twenties. The son, Dylan, studied computer science at a local university. No social media sites."

"That's odd for a twentysomething," Jody said.

Evan agreed.

"We couldn't find a place of residence for him, but that just means he might live at home or with his sister or a roommate."

"Or he doesn't want anyone to see his real identity if he's living a double life and using an alias. If he's a billionaire, then he's stashing luxury items like homes and toys somewhere. He'd have to hide that from his family unless they know about it, which I'm going to say they don't, based on their profile," Jody said. "This guy could be Lawman1."

Evan frowned. "I don't know. It's possible Lawman1—if he's this Dylan Vanhatter—made a mistake and left a trail of two IP addresses, but he might be playing more games. Framing more innocent people for his own twisted reasons."

"This guy is smart and careful. But he is

human, and humans—especially cocky ones—slip up. That IP might be his slip up. And our break," Jody said.

"I'll have August go back and question the head of the gun ring," Wilder said. "They used fake identities to traffic guns. Maybe Lawman1 used the same people to get a fake ID, too."

"Keep us posted." Evan turned his signal on and exited the ramp. "We're going to talk to Layla."

Evan hung up and Jody chewed on the new information. "We might have him."

"Or he might be sending us on yet another chase."

"Let's think positive. I need positive right now."

"Me, too," Evan said.

They pulled up to a modest home in a quiet neighborhood.

"That's Layla's car."

"Doesn't mean anything. She could be here deciding what the next move is." Jody clambered from the vehicle and they knocked on the front door.

It cracked, then Layla swung it open wide. "Agent Novak!" She glanced at Jody. "Jody. What are y'all doin' here?"

"We know the truth, Layla," Evan offered, hoping she'd divulge.

"What truth is that?" she asked, and tucked

a red strand of hair behind her ear. Her brown eyes were shifty.

"Can we come in?"

"Sure."

Evan stepped in first. "You the only one home?"

"For now. My mom's gone to get her hair and nails done." She motioned to the kitchen. Evan followed, wary steps and cautious eyes.

Jody kept her hand on her sidepiece in case Layla was lying and someone else like Lawman1 was lurking. Or was he in Florida? "Can I use the restroom?" She'd snoop and make sure.

"It's down that hall on the left. Y'all want coffee?"

"No, thanks," Evan said.

Lemon. Mothballs. Vanilla—shampoo or lotion—and Layla's floral perfume. Same one she'd smelled in Terry's car that tipped Jody off to the affair.

Jody checked out the three bedrooms, including closets, and finished securing the home before she hobbled back to the kitchen.

Layla was crying.

Guess Evan had cracked her.

Evan folded his arms across his chest. "Layla knows we know about Terry."

"It's horrible. I know. That's why I came to Mama's. I need to figure this out. I'm not a home wrecker. I'm not that person." She grabbed a napkin off the kitchen table and blew her nose.

"Why did you lie to me about SAC Bevin?"

She looked up, wide-eyed. "I didn't lie about anything."

"Layla," Evan said calmly, but his eyes were ice. "You had access to my phone. You overheard the phone call with Terry. If you tell the truth maybe we can lessen your sentence."

"What?" She jumped up. "What sentence? I didn't do anything to your phone and, yes, I overheard, but when is that illegal?"

Evan pursed his lips. "Can I have your phone and laptop?"

"Absolutely."

"Why did you email and tell me not to turn myself in to SAC Bevin because it was a ruse?" Evan took her phone, but kept his cool gaze locked on hers.

"Evan," she said with a shaky voice. "I did not email you and warn you of anything at any time. I love my job. And I follow protocol. I never believed you did what they said, but I need my job."

Evan ground his teeth. Jody stepped in.

"Layla, think. Did you tell anyone else what you overheard from Evan and Terry's phone call?" It was possible Layla's email was hacked—if she was telling the truth. But someone had to personally know about the safe house and Jody's hospitalization.

Layla wiped her nose and shook her head.

"No!" She suddenly froze. "Wait. Yes…but, I mean, there's no way."

Evan leaned forward. "Who did you tell, Layla?"

FOURTEEN

Evan might as well have been sucker punched.

Zoey Wyatt.

Jody scrolled through her phone as they drove back from Layla's mom's house. "She might be lying. They framed you. Framed me. Why not frame Zoey, too? They might even be framing this Dylan Vanhatter guy."

Evan didn't answer her. He was too busy trying to wrap his brain around the fact that sweet and shy Zoey Wyatt might be in cahoots with a mastermind to murder Evan and Jody.

"Now that you're cleared," she asked, "will you be heading back to Washington? The promotion?"

The promotion. He hadn't thought about it in days. Everything was topsy-turvy. "I don't know, Jo. I feel sixteen again."

Unsure. Afraid. Insecure.

Jody shifted in the seat. "You'd be good, especially now that you're not drinking or partying."

Never again. But how could she say this knowing he would eventually be climbing toward her dashed dreams? She was more than he ever deserved. "Thank you." Evan's eyes stung and a lump grew in his throat. When he gained composure, he spoke. "I know I've been working toward this, but sometimes I don't feel like I deserve it."

Jody leaned her head on the seat. "Evan, we can't change the past. I know Christine was never the same after what happened, but she didn't choose to let God help her rise from the ashes. I know it wasn't His fault she was hurt or that I was demoted. And I chose to cover up what happened that night with you. I thought I was protecting you, and I wasn't. I was breaking protocol and probably would have lost my job if I had thrown you to the wolves."

"That's why you didn't tell them I'd been drinking." But she'd lost her job anyway.

"I didn't believe they'd listen. I figured they'd sweep it under the rug. Take care of their boy. Because that's what happened before. But maybe they wouldn't have. Either way, I was wrong. I know that now. I was too angry and hurt to see it before."

"You amaze me."

"Well, I don't know about all that, but don't not take the promotion because you feel bad about what happened to me. It wasn't all your fault.

I can admit that since I decided to get back on board and talk to God again." She grinned, but there was still pain in her eyes.

She'd lost everything. Never been reinstated. He'd realized that earlier today when it sank in that there was something he could do to right the injustice done to her.

It would destroy his career. His reputation. Bring humiliation. Everything he'd worked hard for and feared losing. These things had made him who he was.

His phone dinged. Jody glanced over. "You got a Scripture verse." She chuckled.

"Read it to me. I'm driving."

She picked up his phone. "This thing secure for real now?"

"Yes. After they cleared my name, they issued me a new phone and I made sure to double-check the encryption."

"'Therefore if any man be in Christ, he is a new creature: old things are passed away; behold, all things are become new.' *Second Corinthians* 5:17. I need this app."

It was as if God was answering Evan with a personal text!

He could face the future no matter what. It was like God had given him new DNA—a new creation.

Evan knew exactly what he needed to do. As soon as they brought down Lawman1 and the people helping him, he'd come clean. Clear Jody's name. If she wanted the chance to go back into the Secret Service, he'd make sure she had it. He should have done it years ago, but she was right. He had been selfish. And afraid.

He turned into a small neighborhood. It was after six. Zoey ought to be home. She left work each day by five thirty.

"You know she had the same opportunity to mess with your personal items as Layla. Or Terry."

"I know."

They knocked on the door. Zoey may or may not be home. The garage door was down. No car in the drive.

After the third knock, movement sounded in the house and she opened the door.

"We have some talking to do, Zoey," Evan said.

Jody sniffed. Nodded to Evan.

She smelled something he couldn't. Something that let her know Zoey was either guilty of something or hiding something. After all these years, he could still read Jody's eyes.

"You're alive," Zoey said. "How?"

"Cut the act. Layla told me she filled you in on the truth. I know you planted spyware on my phone and installed a tracking chip in my wallet. I also know you're working with Lawman1 and told him about the safe house, about Jody in the hospital. Why would you think I wouldn't find out?" Evan hardened his tone. Went in as if he already knew it all when he wasn't sure of anything.

Her bottom lip trembled.

"I smell fear," Jody said.

If only Zoey knew how literal Jody was being. Evan smelled nothing.

Zoey's eyes filled with tears and she dropped her head. "How did you find out?"

So it was Zoey.

"I'm gonna be the one to ask the questions here. Who is Lawman1?"

Zoey sniffed. "I don't know. Honestly. I got an email to my private account about a year ago."

"I want your laptop."

She nodded. "He knew about my college loans and credit card debt. I'm drowning in it. He offered me a large amount of Bitcoin and a way to have it exchanged into cash legally and under the radar if I supplied him with some simple answers."

"Such as?" Evan balled his fist. Why hadn't she come to him? He could have helped her figure a way out of her debts.

"What is Evan working on? Who is Evan working with? Is he seeing anyone? Seemingly harmless things, so I accepted the offer. But then when I told him you were heading a new task force to take down the Arsenal, it changed. He changed."

Evan had made a name for himself in the cyber world. Enough that it had garnered Lawman1's attention to keep tabs on him. Until it directly affected him. Hearing Evan had targeted Lawman1's website had set the ball rolling.

"He wanted private information like your username and those involved. I said no, Evan. But I was too far in and he blackmailed me."

Evan raked his hand through his hair. "And you kept him up-to-date on what was happening in the task force?"

She nodded.

"You told him about the sting in the junkyard with the gun dealers and he leaked it to them?" Evan asked, trying to keep calm. She could have gotten everyone killed.

"I did, but I didn't want to."

"You put the spyware on my phone?"

She nodded again.

"Picked the lock on my desk drawer and placed the tracking chip in my wallet?"

"Yes," she whimpered.

"How did you get a high-tech chip like that Zoey?"

"He sent it to me. I have the box. If you want it."

"I do."

They followed her inside and he took the box

from her, his mind whirling. Postal code from Florida. "Why did you call and warn me not to come in that morning?"

"He didn't want you to come in. He wanted you dead. I didn't. You have to believe that!"

Evan wasn't sure what to believe. "And the information Layla gave you—when she thought she was soothing you. When she told you I was alive and at a safe house. You gave that information to Lawman1, as well?"

"I did. I was afraid if I didn't and he found out you were alive and I'd known all along, he'd kill me for withholding information! He knows everything!"

That meant she gave him the information about Jody being in the hospital. His temper ratcheted to explosive levels.

"You know you're under arrest, don't you?" Jody asked.

Zoey buckled at the knees. "I just wanted to pay off my debt."

"Now you have a debt to pay back to society," Evan said. "Zoey Wyatt, you're under arrest…"

Eight hours ago, Evan had arrested Zoey Wyatt but had taken Jody's advice to keep his exoneration quiet for now. If Lawman1 thought Evan was still a fugitive and unable to concentrate on him, he might slip up, and it gave them the advantage. SAC Bevin had met them at a secure location and Evan had briefed him on everything. He wasn't happy, but he understood since they'd been friends a long time. He had taken Zoey into custody and assured Evan they would keep things quiet and give him the time necessary to see this through.

While Evan and Jody had met with SAC Bevin, the FBI had made a deal with Ramos and he'd coughed up the name of the identity theft ring he used. They'd been referred to him through none other than Lawman1. And if Lawman1 had been using them, then they would surely find his real identity and his false one. For the last two hours Evan had been sitting at CCM searching the database with Jody, Wilder, Beckett and Wheezer, but nothing had popped for any of them. It was unbelievable how many people used false identities.

Jody worked across from him, brow furrowed, then she looked up. "Evan. You need to see this."

Her tone and eyes sent a ripple of uneasiness through him. "Did you find him?" She'd found something she didn't like.

Dread and compassion twisted her lips. "Yes… and no."

Evan slowly came around the table and peered over her shoulder into Dylan Vanhatter's face. Dylan Vanhatter, who had purchased an identity that included a fake passport, license and a fake social security number, all under the same alias.

"You recognize him?" Wilder asked.

Evan couldn't speak. Couldn't breathe.

It all flashed in his mind.

"It's Sam Bass," Jody offered quietly. "He's a young man Evan's been mentoring at church—plays basketball on his league."

Evan couldn't believe it. Couldn't force a single syllable out. It was like his lungs had deflated and his ticker stopped ticking.

Jody spoke, but it felt muffled. Too much blood pounding in his ears.

"Wheezer, search the alias. Let's find amenities, bank accounts and homes. Whatever you can pull up, do it. Turn over every rock. I want everything on Sam Bass. I want it yesterday. Evan?"

He couldn't talk about it and stumbled from the room, overwhelmed. Stunned. Sick.

Sam/Dylan had dropped that six-month AA chip six months ago right in front of Evan as a ploy to secure Evan's attention, time and empathy. Evan had poured himself out to Sam Bass. To Dylan. Whoever. He had worked to keep him on the straight and narrow. He'd become someone special to him.

Lunches.

Dinners.

Basketball games.

He'd been in Evan's home! He would've known about his security cameras. Could have easily given that information to the assassin who'd sneaked onto his property. He knew about Jody. Not by name. Evan had never mentioned it, but he'd told him about the woman he'd always loved but hurt. It would only take a little snooping for Sam to find out who Jody was and put two and two together—that she'd taken the blame for Evan's drinking. Sam had toyed with Evan. With Jody. Like a little sign that Lawman1 was right under Evan's nose.

And he had been.

Sam had a traveling job.

Lies.

He said that so he could easily go wherever he kept his toys and home with the money he'd made from commissions of gun sellers. Those two weeks Evan couldn't get in touch with him and was scared out of his mind Sam had fallen off the wagon… He'd worried in vain. Sam was off partying it up. Living his alternate life.

When Evan wouldn't talk about his work, Sam had employed Zoey. Probably combed through everyone's financials and social media sites until he found the perfect victim.

She'd been vulnerable. Needy. Desperate to dig out of debt.

But that wasn't the worst part of it. It only hammered home further how much Evan's betrayal of Jody had destroyed her. Sam had been a man Evan was mentoring. Evan had been the man Jody wanted to marry! He collapsed on the bench in the foyer, hanging his head between his knees. If he could go back… *God, I wish I could go back.*

"Evan?"

Jody.

He couldn't even look at her.

"Evan, I know you're hurt."

Of course she did!

Hurt morphed into anger. He'd been taken advantage of. Lied to. Humiliated. He wanted to put a fist through Sam Bass's face. To put cuffs on him and haul him into a cage for the rest of his life. He rose to his feet and strode into the conference room, Jody following. "I'm going over there. He doesn't know I'm onto him, exonerated or that Zoey is incarcerated. I want to look him in the eye and *personally* arrest him."

"Then I'm going, too." Jody touched his shoulder. "But you need to get a grip on your feelings or you might do something stupid."

He wasn't sure how to do that.

God, help me simmer down. Keep me grounded. Help me do the right thing.

"Beckett and I will come, too," Wilder said. "This guy is calculating and dangerous, with unlimited resources due to dark web connections and more cash than we can count. Jody, you're not at one hundred percent yet or I'd say have at it. We'll stay invisible."

He collected his keys.

They could come up with an idea on the drive back to Macon. An hour and a half later, Wilder had dropped Evan and Jody off at Evan's house so they could drive separately. The game plan was formed.

"Ready?" Evan asked.

"Yep."

He texted Sam: Hey, man, you doing okay? I need a favor.

Sam texted back: Dude. U all over the TV. What is going on?

Evan's blood raced, but he texted back: I can explain. But me and my girl need a place to lay low. Lot to ask but I need somewhere no one would think to look for us. I didn't do what they say I did.

A second later Sam texted back: Yeah, man. I owe you. Anything. Come on.

"Showtime. He bought it."

They drove to Sam's modest apartment, Wilder and Beckett not far behind. Evan cut the engine. "Let's do this." They climbed to the second floor, Jody only wincing once.

Evan knocked.

No answer.

He knocked again. "He knows we're coming."

"Maybe that's not a good thing."

"There's no way he knows anything." Evan twisted the knob. "It's unlocked."

Jody frowned. "Foul play, or is he setting us up to come in? Without a warrant, we could ruin a lot. He could say we didn't have permission."

True. And he could hack the phones and delete the texts, too—even if he needed to delete them from the mainframe at their service provider.

The apartment door across the hall opened and a sweet elderly woman came out, a bag of coffee in her hands. "You must be Sam's guests."

Evan frowned.

"He called and said friends were coming over and he was out of coffee. I told him I'd run it by since I was on my way out."

Coffee. Oh, yeah. They had him good. Relief washed over Evan. "That's us. We can take it in." Give him an additional surprise.

"Oh, how sweet of you." She handed him the bag of coffee and hobbled down the stairs to the parking lot.

"Shall we?" Evan asked.

"We shall." Jody opened the door and they stepped inside.

"Sam?" Evan called as they headed for the kitchen. "Got the coffee. Sam?"

Evan looked around. "You hear that?"

"Shower. That's odd. He knew we were coming over."

Evan's hairs rose on his arms and he drew his weapon. "I don't like it." He crept down the hall.

"Sam?" He put his hand on the doorknob. "Cover me," he whispered.

Evan slowly turned the knob. Two clicking noises sent a wave of nausea through his system.

Jody sniffed. Sniffed again. "I smell something. Can't place it."

"I can." Evan's throat turned dry.

Lawman1 was once again a step ahead of him. Used the old lady to make him and Jody feel safe to enter. Ran the shower as a ploy. He knew Evan would try to open the bathroom door. But who'd tipped him off?

"Jo, I need you to get out of here. He knew we were onto him."

"Why?" She looked at the knob. "Why aren't you letting go of that?"

He didn't need to answer. The sheer terror in her eyes told him she already guessed.

If he moved or let go, the bomb would detonate and they'd both be dead.

FIFTEEN

Jody's body went into rigor mortis.

Evan had activated a bomb!

He stood statuesque. "Jo, get out of here. I don't know how big this thing is. Call SWAT, but do it from outside and stay out there. Cell signals might trigger it."

What? He wanted her to leave him? *Now?* "I'm not going anywhere, but we don't have time to fight about it. Beckett's a bomb expert. I'll find him and call SWAT." She ran outside, her fingers trembling as she made the necessary calls, then she ignored his wishes and came back inside the apartment.

"I thought I told you—"

"Save it. You're not going to stand here alone. Beckett's suiting up. He's down the street so it'll be a minute. SWAT might make it here first."

How long did they have? Her stomach knotted, dipped and dived. When she'd said they were done with each other, this wasn't what she had in mind. He'd still be alive and well.

Sweat dotted Evan's forehead, but he kept his hand in perfect position, holding the knob in a halfway turn. If he moved even a millimeter… "If you ever loved me, Jo, you'd leave."

"Not fair," she said. "Beckett's coming. He can get you out of this. The bomb squad will get you out of this."

"We don't know what *this* is, hon. But if you refuse to leave—" Evan's breath was shaky "—you can listen." His voice cracked. "'Dear Jody…'"

What was he doing?

"'I gave my heart to Jesus this morning.'"

The letter she'd destroyed—he was reciting it from memory. "Evan, you don't have to do this. I forgave you."

He sniffed. "'I had no idea how unsettled my life was…how much I was missing until this amazing peace washed over me as I knelt at the altar. And I cried. For the second time in my adult life.'"

Jody bit the inside of her bottom lip.

"'The first time was the morning you were let go from the Secret Service. When I was supposed to be there with you. By your side, like I promised. But something you probably don't know about me, Jo, that I've tried to hide well, is that I'm a coward.'"

Her lip trembled and she chomped down harder. He was not a coward.

"'That fear has always been a part of me. Fear of becoming my father. Fear of failing the people I love like he did. Fear of never being good enough. Fear of what people thought about me.'"

"Evan," she breathed, and glanced at the door. "Beckett should be here soon."

"'That fear kept me from coming to your aid. I convinced myself that you'd lose your job anyway and so would I. But mostly, I kind of hoped you'd leave me. Every time we argued about marriage—part of me thought you'd leave and then I wouldn't be able to repeatedly hurt you like my dad hurt me and my mom... I can't be that husband or dad. But every time you continued to stick by me. To love me anyway. You're the real hero, Jo. Everything I've ever wanted to be.'" His eyes filled with moisture. "'You're fearless.'"

Jody covered her face with her hands, holding back strangled cries. She was standing here helpless. Fearless? She was scared to death. Tremors ran through her skin.

"'I hope becoming a man of faith will change me. I fear it won't. So I'm not coming back for you. In case it doesn't stick. But even if I never see you again, know that I'm thinking of you with every single breath and working to be a man you'd deserve. A man you can be proud of.'"

The mountain in her throat ached and burned, growing tighter by the second. "Evan…"

"'I hope someday you'll find it in yourself to forgive me for what I did. I'll regret it every day.'" Evan closed his eyes, slowly inhaled. When he opened them he gave her a smile that held sorrow and more sincerity than she'd ever seen from one person. "'Always yours, Evan.'"

But he wasn't hers. She'd pushed him away for fear of getting hurt once again.

"Jo, I can't go to my grave—"

"No one is going to their grave!" He wasn't dying. They would make it out…and then what? She swiped tears away. Wished to wipe his away, too, but they dripped from his chin onto his shirt.

"Jo, I love you. I have always loved you—the best I could with what I had. I'm sorry I wasn't there for you in the hospital. I should have been. You were right. I was thinking of me even when I was thinking of you. And I do think of you. I use the laundry detergent that reminds me of you. I even keep a jar of vapor rub by my bed… I'm pitiful." He half laughed and eyed the knob.

"Evan," she managed to say, and bent at the knees.

"Please go. Live your life and live it with someone who will make you laugh and never hurt you."

That wasn't possible, was it? People hurt and hurt people. No one was perfect. Evan had done what he thought was best and it had been a mistake. Instead of offering him grace, she'd cocooned her heart, her previous fears and insecurities holding her back. She moved toward him.

"Stop!"

She froze.

"I can't chance you coming any closer." He closed his eyes. His hand shook. "I don't know how much longer I can keep this position. My hand is sweating and cramping."

"You hold on! Do you hear me?" He couldn't give up. Blood whooshed in her ears. Time was literally ticking.

"Jody?"

Beckett. In full SWAT gear. "I got here fast as I could. You need to leave the premises. SWAT ought to be here—"

Here now.

"Evan?" Beckett asked. "How many clicks did you hear when you turned the knob?" He glanced back at Jody. "Go right now or I'm going to personally remove you, and I won't be nice or gentle about it."

"Ma'am, you need to leave," the SWAT commander said. "Marsh."

"Reed." Beckett nodded. Did the man know every bomb expert?

"Where's Wilder?" Jody asked.

"He's on the hunt for Vanhatter. Go help him."

Leave now? It might be crazy, but she wanted to stick this out. To whatever end it may be. "I'm fine right here."

Beckett growled and turned to Evan. "Clicks?"

"Two," Evan answered.

The SWAT team members were already cutting out the wall into the bathroom.

Beckett frowned. "Sounds like one click activated the bomb. The second click set a timer in place."

Metal, iron and drywall dust reached her nose as they continued to drill. Evan mouthed for her to leave, but she shook her head.

"We're in." A SWAT team member stepped into the bathroom.

"What do we have?" Beckett asked.

"I don't know. I haven't seen anything like this before." Beckett and the SWAT commander stepped into the bathroom for several seconds and then stepped out.

"Okay, Evan. We have something new," Beckett said. "The first click set it in motion and the second click recorded your body temperature. And that temp, 99.2, is our regulator. I can't be sure how far above or below it can go before it blows. Maybe one degree. Maybe it has to stay regulated. I've never encountered this."

The world tilted. How were they going to keep his body temperature regulated?

"And if you let go of the knob or twist it at all

from where it is now, it blows." Beckett's grim expression sent a ripple of terror through Jody's bones.

"Building is cleared," a team member said over the radio.

"My hand is sweating." Evan held Beckett's somber gaze.

"Somebody get me some cooling packs!" Beckett barked. A SWAT member returned with one.

"And a lighter in case his temp drops," the SWAT commander—Reed—added. "Evan, take deep breaths. Focus. Bring your body temp down."

"It's 99.3…4…" the member monitoring the temperature gauge called out.

"My heart's racing, man."

"Breathe," Beckett said. "Find something we can use as a pulley. If we can attach it to the doorknob and keep it twisted, we could tie it off on the bedroom doorknob and then maybe use a lighter…no…" He growled. "I need something I can use for heat but won't turn off. A lighter isn't going to do it."

"Hair dryer!" Jody said. "You can turn it on low. Use a thermometer to gauge how far back from the knob it needs to be to mimic 99.2. You can hang it on something to secure it."

"Good thinking, Jo," Evan said.

SWAT members scrambled for items. Beckett removed the ice packs from Evan's hand. "Temp?"

The SWAT member in the bathroom called back, "Ninety-nine point one."

"You can't go below 99, Evan. I have a bad feeling," Beckett said.

"Found these exercise cords. We can use them as resistance to hold the doorknob in place."

"Here's the hair dryer."

"So he's going to be okay?" Jody asked.

"We're MacGyverin' it here, Jode. I don't know if this will work at all."

Evan's expression curdled her blood.

He knew he wasn't making it out alive.

"Okay, we got it all in place."

"Ninety-nine point seven…"

"Cold packs!" Beckett barked. "Evan, breathe!"

"Ninety-nine point eight…"

The SWAT commander stepped up. "Everyone clear out."

Beckett heaved a breath. "When it's clear, Evan, you won't have much time. The hair dryer will increase the temperature. You only have a few seconds to let go so the dryer can hold the right temperature without your body heat raising it. You do that and get out." They put a helmet with a face shield on his head.

"How much time do I have once I let go?"

"If the resistance stays the same and the hair dryer keeps the temp at 99.2, all the time you need. If it doesn't…" He clasped his shoulder. "I'm praying for you, man."

Evan nodded.

Beckett touched Jody's shoulder, his voice low. "It's time to say your goodbyes, Jody."

Goodbyes?

"What? No!" Speech wouldn't come. Spots formed before her eyes.

The hair dryer hummed.

SWAT members mumbled in muted tones.

"Jo," Evan whispered. "Go. Be smart. This time…this time it's braver to leave than stay."

"I don't care. I don't want to be a hero. I want to stay here. With you."

Evan sighed. "Then come here. Kiss me."

She inched toward him and lightly placed her lips on his. Didn't matter that Beckett stood watching. Didn't matter a bomb was about to take them into eternity.

She had right now. And she was going to savor his scent of cinnamon and citrus—the taste of their salty tears mixing together and the familiar taste of Evan.

"I love you, Jo," he whispered against her lips.

She opened her eyes in time to see Evan give one resolute nod to Beckett. "Do it," he said.

Before she could blink, Beckett thrust Jody over his shoulders like a sack of potatoes, her leg screaming in pain, but she ignored it as tears blurred her vision. She beat his back and hollered for him to let her go. "Put me down! You can't do this!" Her throat ached and burned. "We can't leave him! *Evan!*"

Beckett didn't speak. He toted her down the stairs and outside the hot zone. But he gripped her like iron. She couldn't break free.

"I'm fine. I am. You can put me down now." Lies. All lies.

He released her from over his shoulders but kept his grip around her waist, holding her in a prison from behind.

"You can let go." She couldn't break free from his hold.

"You'll run right back in there for him if I do. Been there. Done that." He gripped her chin and made her face him. "We've lost enough lives in the Flynn family. Do you understand?"

Grandparents. Her father. *Meghan.* She understood. But still. "Beckett!" she pleaded. *"Please!"*

He turned her toward him and buried her face in his chest. "Don't watch this."

Maybe it worked. Evan would come running from the apartment complex. Safe. Sound.

Jody screamed into his vest as the sonic boom deafened her.

The building blew with a fiery blast. Smoke clouded the atmosphere; debris showered down.

And Evan was gone.

* * *

"We got something! Over here!"

Evan couldn't move. Something heavy weighted him down. He coughed inside the helmet. His throat was coated in grit. Ears ringing, he couldn't make out the voices.

Have. To. Move.

Jody! Was she safe?

The fuzziness in his head cleared some and he remembered letting go of the knob, the exercise band working to keep it twisted at the right degree. The hair dryer doing its job. He'd raced from Dylan's apartment and down the stairs when the blast sent him sprawling into the air.

Debris had rained down on him, then everything had gone black. He wasn't sure how long he'd been out, but it felt like he'd been hollering forever.

"Evan! Can you hear me, man?"

Wilder's voice.

"I'm…under… I'm here. Wilder!" Evan was pinned by whatever had landed on him. A door? Bricks. Railing.

Remains shifted. "We got ya," Wilder said, and grunted as the heavy weight was lifted from him. "Finally. We been hunting through the rubble for a while now."

First responders came to his aid. "Sir, don't move."

"I'm fine." He removed the SWAT helmet and surveyed the scene. The whole complex was gone.

"Look a little on the bloody side to me," Wilder said, and grinned. "Welcome back to the land of the living."

"Where's Jo?" Evan asked as the paramedics took his vitals and annoyed him. He was fine. He just wanted to get to Jo.

"Well, at first she tried to go back in after you, but Beck wouldn't let her. Then she tried to claw through debris to hunt you down, but when Beckett dished out his tough love, her leg was reinjured." He held up his hand. "She's fine. We basically had to act as straitjackets to get her to the hospital. They fixed her up but pumped her with the sleepy pills."

"Where is she?"

"She's at your place. Snoozing. And probably dreaming of all the ways she's gonna kill us when she wakes up. Cosette and Beckett's wife, Aurora, drove in and are with her now."

Evan stood. "Do I need stitches?"

"No, minor scrapes and abrasions. You're blessed not to have any major wounds," the paramedic said. "We'd like to take you to the hospital for further evaluation."

"Nope. I'm fine." Nothing a few ibuprofens wouldn't fix. "I need to get home."

To Jody.

"There you are!" SAC Bevin hurdled broken concrete and bricks and rushed to him. Terry

Pratt was right behind him. "We've been going crazy looking for you."

Terry held out his hand. "No hard feelings?"

Evan grinned and hugged him. "I'm sorry."

"I'd have done the same thing, man." Terry slapped his back and released him. Evan couldn't say if he and Layla would pick back up—he hoped not. He hoped Terry would come clean and reconcile with his wife.

"Got the call from Washington," Clive said. "It's yours, Evan. Assistant Director of Protective Operations. You've brought down three different criminal rings in one investigation. I'll be sorry to see you go."

Wilder gave him a sideways glance.

"Thank you," he said. But he wasn't so sure he wanted or even needed that position anymore. His perspective had changed in the past several days. What he'd once thought was important didn't have the same shine it had before.

"Reporters are going nuts. We need to give a press conference and reinstate you publicly. Why don't you get cleaned up and we can meet back in an hour at the agency. Let's tell the world what you've done."

He'd be at that press conference all right.

And he planned to tell the world exactly what he'd done. "Be there in an hour." Evan hobbled to Wilder's SUV and climbed inside. "He said three rings. Did they get Sam?"

"Dylan Vanhatter, you mean?" Wilder asked. "Yeah. We got him. He was boarding a chartered plane heading to Morocco. Looks like Fenner's team sent FBI to question the Vanhatters. They said Dylan lived with a girlfriend near Miami and traveled for his job. They only saw him occasionally." He snorted. "Also living as Sam Bass in sweet digs a few hours from them."

And getting an apartment here to keep tabs on Evan. To toy with him. He came and went under the guise of a traveling job. He'd fooled them all. "They called him after the FBI left. That's how he was onto us, wasn't it?"

"Yep. The guy is resourceful. I'll give him that."

He'd likely had dozens of contingency plans. Including Morocco. "No extradition laws."

"Exactly. But he wasn't counting on you having extra backup, and Wheezer was on it the second I called him—when Jody came down and told us what had happened in the apartment. He figured out where Dylan was heading."

"I owe that guy…something." Evan chuckled.

"Dylan's computers and devices gave analysts what they needed to freeze his online wallets so he couldn't spend any Bitcoin. He's going away for a long, long time."

"Good." Evan thought he wanted to be the one to take him in personally, to look him in the face, but after everything that had transpired all Evan cared about now was that he was going away and couldn't hurt anyone else. And of course Jody.

He was alive, and if this wasn't an opportunity for a second chance, he didn't know what was. They entered Evan's house. Cosette met them at the door.

"She awake?" Wilder asked.

"No." She turned to Evan. "I'm glad you're okay... *Evan*."

Not Agent Novak anymore. He grinned. "Where is she?"

"Guest room bed."

He strode to the guest room. Jody was lying in the middle of the bed, hair rumpled and sleeping. She wasn't only physically beautiful. She had the most beautiful inside. This woman would have gone to the grave with him. Not the smartest idea but loyal. If she was willing to stick that out with him, she might be willing to stick out the rest of her life with him, even if he did make mistakes. Which he would. But if they could get through what he'd done in the past and through everything that had happened in the past week and a half then surely, with God, they could get through anything.

He brushed her hair back from her face and she shifted, winced. Must be in pain. Leaning down, he pressed a kiss to her forehead. "I love you, you wild, crazy, wonderful woman." He studied her a moment longer—it was so hard to break away from her. Then he kissed her once more on the lips and left to clean up for the press conference.

At the front door, he turned to Cosette. "If you can coax her awake in the next thirty minutes, please do. I want her to see the press conference."

Cosette patted his arm. "I'll do my best." She looked at Wilder. "And when we get back to CCM—"

"I'm taking a nap, then eating a steak dinner."

"Wilder…at some point you have to talk to me."

"I'm talking to you right now."

"Wilder Flynn!" She popped her hands on her hips and frowned.

Wilder laughed and opened the door. "Come on, I'll drive you to the press conference." He closed the door on Cosette and walked to the SUV.

"Why does she want to talk to you?" Evan asked as he buckled up.

"She makes everyone at CCM do a weekly session with her. Mental health. Blah-blah."

"So talk to her."

Wilder snorted. "Cosette doesn't just talk. She gets all up in your head and under your skin." He shuddered. "I don't need that."

Evan kept silent. None of his business. Fifteen minutes later they arrived at the Secret

Service Agency. The press littered the front of the building.

"Go time. Looks like, Washington, here you come." Wilder pocketed his keys.

Evan studied him. Wilder was baiting him. Evan grinned. "I'm not going to Washington. Everything I want is in Atlanta."

"What about a job?"

"I haven't got that far yet." Right now, he had to make things right then see how Jody felt about marrying him.

Wilder grinned. "Ever thought of private security?"

"Are you offering me a job?"

"Yeah, but it's contingent on what my cousin has to say when you get gooey on her."

Shaking his head, Evan laughed again. "You never been gooey on anyone?"

"I don't have that luxury. But I envy those of you who do."

Evan frowned. "You can love someone and be in a dangerous job. Everyone on your team pretty much does."

"I'm not talking about loving someone, Novak."

"What *are* you talking about then?"

Wilder pointed to the door. "Out ya go. If she says yes, come find me and fill out the paperwork."

"And if she says no?" Evan asked.

Smirking, Wilder shrugged. "I guess you hit the road, Jack."

Evan closed the SUV door and headed for the reporters, who were already begging for the scoop. But Evan didn't respond. Praise from men was no longer a draw. He didn't need their respect or admiration.

He only wanted that from one woman.

He shook hands with Clive and took the podium.

SIXTEEN

"He was here and left?" Jody clutched her chest. Evan was alive. He'd made it out! She pressed her palms to her burning eyes. A relieved and thankful sob erupted and her head swam due to the pain meds. She was now nestled on the couch, elated and awaiting the news Cosette had woken her up to watch.

Cosette grinned and handed her a cup of tea and a tissue. "Don't get upset."

Jody laughed. "I'm not. I'm just relieved he's alive." She sipped the tea. "Besides, he lives here, so he'll be back at some point." And she needed the rest. "I'm still upset with Beckett and Wilder. And they know it. That's why they've made themselves scarce."

Cosette switched on the TV and turned it up. "Beckett and Aurora drove back after Evan was found. Wilder drove him to the press conference, though I have a feeling that has nothing to do with being scarce around you, but me."

"He'll talk when he's ready."

"He'll never be ready. But let's talk about you. You and Evan."

Jody grinned. "I don't know. He loves me. I believe that. But I don't know if I can go back to Washington after everything. Not that I blame Evan anymore. It's…awkward. What would I do? I can't go back into the agency. I'm pretty much alienated there. And Evan deserves this promotion, so if he takes it and then he wants me to move to Washington with him—married or in separate apartments—I'll do it. For him. I'll figure something out. But I'll do it."

"Press conference is starting."

Cosette had filled her in on Dylan Vanhatter's arrest, as well. "I'm happy for Evan. He looks good up there, doesn't he?"

"He does. He's handsome for sure."

Evan came on-screen wearing a navy blue suit with a powder blue dress shirt. His tie was a mix of both colors, bringing out his eyes.

"I want to thank you for coming out," he said with quiet authority. "Today, ghost guns have been taken out of the reach of criminals. Identity theft and gun rings have fallen and Dylan Vanhatter, aka Sam Bass aka Lawman1, has been taken into custody and his dark website, the Arsenal, has been deactivated. It's a good, good day today. But I didn't do this alone." He acknowledged his task force and Covenant Crisis

Management, one by one each team member and how they'd contributed to the mission, as well as Beckett Marsh saving his life.

"I guess I can't stay mad at Beck forever," Jody teased. He'd done it for her own good. She sipped her tea as Evan continued.

"But one member of CCM deserves a special acknowledgment. Three years ago, Secret Service Agent Jody Gallagher was fired after evidence showed she'd been drinking on the job and allowing security to be breached by the press."

Jody's hand shook and her tea sloshed over the side. Cosette took it from her.

"The truth is Jody was protecting another agent. An agent who had been fully responsible for that breach of security. I know this firsthand…"

Evan, don't! You'll wreck your career. Everything you worked for. You've been forgiven and you have this amazing opportunity.

"Because I was that agent. I let her take the fall to save my career. And I've regretted it every day."

Reporters hurled questions over one another in a frenzy.

"With that, I'm resigning from my position at the Secret Service. I will not be accepting a promotion to Assistant Director of Protective Operations in Washington, DC. The most qualified person for that job is Jody Gallagher. If anyone deserves it, it's her."

Jody's chest tightened; tears burned her eyes. She had no words. He'd sacrificed everything. For her.

Evan slipped from the podium.

The news would be filled with talk of Evan. That night would be rehashed all over again. It killed Jody but not for herself. She'd endured it and come out stronger. God hadn't given up on her. He'd been working on her all this time. Quietly but tenderly.

But Evan would have to face his biggest fears. Some might respect his honesty and let the fact that he'd brought down three crime rings speak for itself, but there would be naysayers. He'd lose respect and admiration from colleagues.

"He loves you, Jody. So much." Cosette carried the tea to the kitchen, and in a few minutes the door opened and Evan and Wilder bounded inside.

Cosette looked from Evan to Jody. "Wilder," Cosette said.

"What?" he said through a groan, and threw his head back like a child who knew he was about to be told to clean his room.

Scowling, Cosette nodded toward Jody and Evan. "How about we go get that steak and take our hour."

He frowned, then tossed out his signature

smile that oozed charm and grace. The same grin that had gotten him out of whuppings as a kid. He extended his arm for Cosette to loop hers into. "You know, Cosette, I have a better idea. I saw this sweet little crawfish joint not far from here. How about we get our gumbo on, instead."

"Wooeee." She laid on the thick Cajun accent and took his arm. "I like that idea, *mon cher*."

He chuckled and they left Jody standing by the couch, facing Evan.

"I'd come running into your arms, but I kinda can't." Jody laughed and cried. "You scared me to death today."

"Are you going to hold it against me forever, like you said you would when I almost drowned?" His mischievous smile undid her.

She snickered. "Come here right now."

In two strides, Evan had her in his arms.

"I can't believe you did that, Evan. Why did you do that?" She buried her face into his chest, inhaling his scent, thankful he was here and alive.

"I should have done that a long time ago." He pulled back and raised her chin to peer into his eyes. "You deserved that and so much more. People needed to know."

"But I was okay."

"I wasn't." He caressed her face with his thumb. "When Beckett carried you out of the apartment building, all I could think was how grateful I was to have a last moment with you. A last kiss with you. The last face I got to see was yours. But I had one regret…and that was not declaring to the world what an amazing woman and agent you are. God gave me that chance."

"Evan, I'm sorry. For everything. I love you. I love you whether you did that or not. I just got through telling Cosette I'd make it work even if I had to go to Washington."

He stroked her cheek with his thumb. "Well, you don't have to. Unless you get a call from the agency and want to. And then, I'll go. With you. By *your* side."

She clasped his hands, which cradled her cheeks. "You would do that?"

He claimed her lips with ease and grace. The truth was clear. He would go anywhere with her. Do anything for her. Breaking the kiss, he pecked her nose, then dropped to his knee and pulled a black velvet box from his pocket. "I bought this six months after we started dating— the day after I told you I loved you. Before we did everything wrong and out of order. Before I let fear paralyze me. But you need to know that, Jody. You need to know that I wanted you for a lifetime before I ever even kissed you on our second date. Jody Siobhan Gallagher, will you marry me?"

Jody was stunned, looking at the gorgeous princess-cut diamond on a thick white-gold band. He'd bought her a ring. He'd thought about it. He'd loved her. He'd always loved her. She could hardly find her voice. "Yes," she squeaked. "Yes!"

He slid the engagement ring on her finger and stood, drawing her so far into him she wasn't sure where she ended and he began. "I should tell you something else," he murmured as he peppered her lips with kisses.

"What's that?"

"I was offered a job at CCM."

Jody grinned. Working with Wilder had started out as a fallback from the fallout. But she realized now that working with family and helping people who needed their expertise was what she loved most. She didn't want to go back to the Secret Service and she was sure Granddaddy Flynn would be equally proud of her being right here, right now. "I think we make a pretty great team, Novak."

"I do, too… Novak."

"Jody Novak. Sounds good."

Evan grinned and kissed her again. "No. It sounds perfect."

* * * * *

Dear Reader,

Sometimes we get angry at God when we don't see Him working in our lives—when it feels He's absolutely silent and ignoring us. Jody didn't see justice for a grievous wrong done to her friend or herself, but instead of trusting God to someday make it right, she let a man who wasn't a believer fill her empty and hurting heart. She rebelled against God and made a lot of poor choices. Maybe like Jody, you've made some poor choices due to anger and hurt. Right now you might be far away from God without any clue how to get back into a relationship with Him. Like Jody, all it takes is opening up some dialogue with Him.

Pray.

Ask God to heal and forgive you. He will. You can find peace. Move forward and pursue God's will for your life. He hasn't changed His mind about you. His arms are always open.

I love to connect with readers. Please sign up for my newsletter at www.jessicarpatch.com for contests, giveaways and book news. You can email me at jessica@jessicarpatch.com.

Warmly,
Jessica

Get 2 Free Books,
Plus 2 Free Gifts—
just for trying the Reader Service!

Love Inspired®

LI17R3

Get 2 Free Books,
Plus 2 Free Gifts—
just for trying the
Reader Service!

HOME on the RANCH

YES! Please send me the **Home on the Ranch Collection** in Larger Print. This collection begins with 3 FREE books and 2 FREE gifts in the first shipment. Along with my 3 free books, I'll also get the next 4 books from the Home on the Ranch Collection, in LARGER PRINT, which I may either return and owe nothing, or keep for the low price of $5.24 U.S./ $5.89 CDN each plus $2.99 for shipping and handling per shipment*. If I decide to continue, about once a month for 8 months I will get 6 or 7 more books, but will only need to pay for 4. That means 2 or 3 books in every shipment will be FREE! If I decide to keep the entire collection, I'll have paid for only 32 books because 19 books are FREE! I understand that accepting the 3 free books and gifts places me under no obligation to buy anything. I can always return a shipment and cancel at any time. My free books and gifts are mine to keep no matter what I decide.

268 HCN 3760 468 HCN 3760

Name	(PLEASE PRINT)	
Address		Apt. #
City	State/Prov.	Zip/Postal Code

Signature (if under 18, a parent or guardian must sign)

Mail to the **Reader Service:**

IN U.S.A.: P.O. Box 1867, Buffalo, NY. 14240-1867
IN CANADA: P.O. Box 609, Fort Erie, Ontario L2A 5X3

READERSERVICE.COM

Manage your account online!

- Review your order history
- Manage your payments
- Update your address

We've designed the Reader Service website just for you.

Enjoy all the features!

- Discover new series available to you, and read excerpts from any series.
- Respond to mailings and special monthly offers.
- Browse the Bonus Bucks catalog and online-only exculsives.
- Share your feedback.

Visit us at:
ReaderService.com